CW00549550

1

SNODSBURY HALL, ENGLAND, MARCH, 1958

Lady Mary Culpeper, Duchess of Snodsbury, sighed as she surveyed the lawn and deer park of Snodsbury Hall. A cool mist lay in the hollows of the park, slowly burning off under a watery sun whose warmth could hardly be detected. Water dripped from eaves and the bare tree branches. Snow still visible in shaded places, and elsewhere, among the trees, carpets of snowdrops maintained the wintry aspect.

Mary glanced over at Barkley, a plump royal corgi who snubbed his fuzzy, button nose against the window and snapped his head back at the chill. He tilted his foxy face and stared intently at his lady, as if looking for an explanation. The plump corgi again pressed his damp nose to the glass and huffed. The stump of his tail wagged excitedly. Little oval patches of fog from his breath formed on the glass while his eyes followed a small rabbit hopping outside on the lawn.

A faint thwacking noise reverberated down the paneled hall as Cook pounded a chicken flat for the day's meal. Loud boisterous chatter boomed toward Mary.

"Your Grace, breakfast will chill, and Cook will be upset," Ponsonby stated with a wrinkle in his metaphorical cap.

Ponsonby, Snodsbury Hall's butler and her husband's trusted valet of many years, and Cook, were her oldest and most trusted staff. Their only disagreement, in a long and amicable relationship, was frequently not seeing eye-to-eye on what was good for her.

"She'll be as anxious as a long-tailed cat in a roomful of rocking chairs," Mary replied dryly to her butler, coaxing his deeply furrowed brow back into two separate shapes. The phrase was one they'd recently learned from an American visitor.

Ponsonby's expression softened, and she saw a hint of a smile twitch the side of his lips, a proper smile not able to escape.

The breakfast bell rang twice, and Barkley raised his head in attention.

Mary looked down fondly at her companion skittering back and forth in front of the window and smiled. "Soon enough, Barkley, soon enough," she said, knowing the bunnies didn't have much time left before the corgi was chasing their tails.

The rabbits gave Barkley plenty of excitement, but they filled Mary with homesickness. Why, she couldn't say, but they reminded her of her childhood home in Cheshire. A twinkle formed in her eye, a shimmer of hope brought on by the snow-drops flowering, the first sign of spring here in Norfolk, her home since she and her late husband, the duke, had come into the title upon the death of his father in 1935. That was twenty-three years, and a lifetime ago.

Mary bent to pick up the overweight corgi, who grew heavier with each passing year. He was over two stones now, despite all his chasing. Mary scratched the top of his head.

"We can't upset Cook," Lady Mary finally agreed, answering Ponsonby's earlier notion.

Entering the breakfast room, the last thing on Mary's mind

today was irritating the cook, a fiercely loyal and protective woman. Cook's vexation would not be for the wasted food but for the duchess's lack of appetite. The close knit staff fussed over the duchess like a mother hen, but this morning, the ball of anxiety churning in the pit of Mary's stomach left no room for food. Mary tightened the worn silk belt of her robe, a veiled attempt at an ounce of security.

"No, milady, we must not upset Cook," Ponsonby said, ushering her to a chair at a table much too large for a single person. With Roland gone, and no children, everything in the hall loomed over her.

"I was enjoying this beautiful morning," Mary said, waving toward the bank of floor to ceiling windows. Her smile increased as she continued, "The grounds, especially the bare trees, look so ethereal in the mist, yet somehow, it raises my spirits."

Ponsonby was well aware of why her spirits were down. The early morning mail had brought a letter from Johnson, the estate manager, and Butterell, the estate lawyer, presenting last year's accounts and outlining their suggestions for the Snodsbury estate's future. This missive was to prepare the duchess for their quarterly meeting, a significant drain on Mary as she aged. With the estate no longer paying its way for nearly thirty years, when the Depression had taken hold and constant government demands for taxes and duties had ended any hope of recovery. Their professional advice was always to sell—sell portions of the Snodsbury lands, parceling them out, leaving only a shred of her former life.

"There wasn't better news, milady?" Ponsonby asked. Clearly, her mood was evident.

Mary shook her head at his pointed stare. She detected the dispatch was weighing heavily on *his* mind, as well.

"Pigs may fly, Ponsonby," she finally replied. "When we meet next week, I expect them to tell me I must seek employment."

"I'm sure they wouldn't suggest anything of the sort."

Ponsonby had been her sure place of calm strength these past years.

"I shall suggest the few charity committees I'm on begin to take a salary for what we do. That might help us a little and also some of the other committee members. I have given Your Grace my suggestions before," Ponsonby said while pouring Mary's coffee, "so I'm pleased to hear you are considering one of them." He paused. "If I may speak out of turn once more?"

Mary laughed. "You can never speak out of turn to me, Ponsonby. You know that. Your council has always been appreciated."

He acknowledged her words with a slight nod of his head and continued, "While Mr. Johnson is a good man in every respect, he... How shall I say this? He is not active enough."

"Old Mr. Johnson has been steward of this estate since before we arrived," Mary replied, her words gentle. She added a sugar cube to her coffee, and the silver spoon tinkled as she swirled the dissolving cube.

She shared his view on Johnson. However, loyalty bound them all together. Mary knew exactly what Ponsonby's unspoken opinion was. *Johnson is not clever enough to turn around my failing enterprise.*

"Yes, a younger, more aggressive man with a sharper mind might rescue us." Mary sipped her coffee and added, "But there is the factor of fealty."

Ponsonby began, "Milady..." when a thunderous clank resounded through the walls of the breakfast room. The muscle in Ponsonby's jaw twitched.

Mary smiled and nodded as they were sure thinking the same thing. *Cook.*

"We can talk later, old friend," Mary said. "Neither of us will live to see the future if we delay breakfast any longer."

WITHOUT FURTHER INTERRUPTIONS, Mary finished picking at her breakfast and then returned to her room to prepare for the day. Taking the seat at her vanity, she stared at her reflection. The possibility of selling off more of her former life dragged a frown across her face as she stroked a string of pearls that Roland had purchased for her. The estate, her two staff, a few pieces of jewelry, and her fading memories were all that she had left of her departed husband. Her advisors' advice was to retrench staff and property further and raise tenants' rents.

Speaking to her reflection in the mirror, Mary said, "Everyone is already doing double duty. Ponsonby is butler, driver, and footman, while Cook is cook, reluctant house maid, and, when the occasion arises, lady's maid too."

Her reflection stared impassively back as she continued, "I will not discharge my staff or raise my tenants' rents nor will I fell the tree. Many 'old families' may well be doing it, but I won't."

Mary pondered the trees she'd admired earlier that morning and through the years, ghost-like during the winter season.

A grim expression clouded her otherwise kindly countenance as she whispered to herself, "I've already sold all the family's other estates. There's a mortgage on this property, and now they wish to sell or lease my London house."

Mary sighed, and her shoulders drooped slightly before she recovered her posture. She realized it would come to this, for it often did, but the London house was where she and Roland had lived for most of their early married life. The decision between the two properties would be an impossible choice for her to make.

"Very well," she resigned, glaring at her reflection. "I'll let them entertain bringing in tenants for the London house. They must, however, be the right *sort* of people."

With that, Mary left her room and descended the stairs to the morning room where she returned to her handwork. Resigned to telephone her two tormentors later and set the wheels in motion, she hummed a hollow tune as she stitched embroidered daisy chains on a tablecloth for her bedside table.

Moments later, Ponsonby entered the room and asked, "Does milady need anything right now?" His tone suggested a stiff whisky might be in order.

"No, I'm fine for the time being," Mary replied and continued with her needlework.

Ponsonby cleared his throat and asked, "Did they have *any* new ideas, milady?"

She shook her head. "No, just the same old story. I fear I shall have to seek employment, but for now, I will allow tenants for the London estate," she replied, smiling up at him encouragingly, but a grave feeling washed over her face for a moment, and she knew he saw it.

2

SNODSBURY HALL, ENGLAND, APRIL 1958

The telephone rang, and Mary looked curiously to Ponsonby before he left the room. With the door ajar, she overheard him answer the telephone, and then his echoing footsteps tapped against the wooden floor as he crossed back across the empty hall.

Ponsonby entered the sitting room.

Looking up from her needlework, Mary asked, "Was that the telephone?"

"Yes, milady."

"Who is it?" she asked.

"A secretary from Buckingham Palace, milady," Ponsonby said in a puzzled tone.

"What do they want?" Mary asked, rising to her feet. "They haven't telephoned me in years, not since Roland's..." She stood and set her embroidery down on the seat. "Well, never mind that. I'll take the call."

She strode across the wooden floor with a spring in her step to the waiting telephone in the hall.

Picking up the handset, she said, "Yes. This is Lady Mary."

The voice, a young woman, replied, "This is Eleanor Fortescue, one of the Palace social secretaries. You knew my mother, Lady Fortescue, then Daphne Carruthers, many years ago."

Mary did remember. "How is your mother? We lost touch with the war and..."

She stopped. Roland's death had been such a blow she'd become a bit of a recluse, not leaving the house or entertaining company before falling out of that world altogether.

"She's well, milady," Eleanor said, "and asked me to remember her to you."

"That is kind," Mary said. "We were quite close once."

"Mother has told me so much about the adventures you shared. In fact, that's part of the reason I'm phoning."

"The Palace has an adventure for us?" Mary asked, almost laughing at herself and the change in her mood—utter dejection an hour ago and now something like joy. *Oh, to be useful again.*

Eleanor laughed. "Not exactly, but we do have a commission for you, if you will take it."

"Quite mysterious, tell me," Mary stated and listened closely as Eleanor outlined the proposal. When Eleanor finished speaking, Mary blinked and nodded. "Yes, I see. I understand." Finally, she said, "Yes, of course, I accept."

With a flourish, she set the receiver on the hook before sashaying back to her sitting room. Picking up her needlework, she sat back down in her favorite chair—Roland's chair moved into her sitting room after his passing. She breathed deeply, but the chair no longer carried the familiar scent of his cigars and Scotch, yet it comforted her just the same. She began her stitches with a grin that reached her spirit as well as her face.

Ponsonby re-entered the room. "Milady?"

"It looks as though I'll have a job after all," she said and cocked her head to look at Barkley by the fire. *Good news indeed. An answer to my prayers for certain.*

"Milady?"

"Please contact Butterell and tell him there will be no need to search for renters. We'll be returning to the London house. Please ask him to have it readied before the start of the new week. We'll leave on the Friday train."

"May I share with him the reason why?"

"Ponsonby, the Palace has summoned me to London for this year's presentation of the debutantes. I am to prepare the current group of young ladies for their presentation to the Queen in one months' time at Queen Charlotte's Ball." She laughed and continued, "I trust you'll handle Cook?"

"Yes milady, of course," Ponsonby said, stiffly. "I feel it would be only sensible of me to suggest Cook may wish to speak to you about this sudden removal to town."

Mary laughed. "I'll take lunch here and compliment Cook fulsomely after, in hopes of avoiding her wrath unscathed, particularly when I tell her of all the guests we'll have in London and how her expertise will be vital in supporting my new position. I hope she'll feel additionally valued."

"Very well, milady," Ponsonby said. "You will learn that Cook has only just received what she considers an appropriate delivery of provisions after a long period where none were to be had. May I assure her we will bring them all with us?"

"You may," Mary said. "The moving costs are to be paid by the Palace so she may take as much of everything as she feels she needs."

Ponsonby's frozen expression indicated he doubted this would be enough.

"I'll do my needlework until the afternoon post comes. Then, we shall begin preparing ourselves for London," She said, a new optimism filling her tone and spiriting her rising hopes.

Left with her thoughts, she and Barkley sat companionably by the fire while she practiced new embroidery stitches on an old handkerchief. The firelight shone on his sable-colored coat, and Mary thought how delighted Barkley would be being reunited with his royal corgi cousins. *Oh goodness, he's going to need a diet. He must be trimmed down before his appearance with the Queen. Yes, a diet, he must begin immediately. And what about myself?*

Barkley wasn't the only one who had been slightly spoiled by their long years of rustication in the country. Mary sighed audibly, and the dog perked up one ear and then went gingerly back to sleep. She reached down and gently stroked his head, unable to stop smiling at this new position the Queen was offering. The mere thought of returning to the London house for several weeks set her heart beating wildly.

As so often happened, her happiness was instantly filled with nostalgia, though something else stirred in her mind. In her mid-fifties, could she really prepare the young ladies of today for their debutante ball? Especially when she was so long since removed from the pomp and circumstance of the Palace and Royals?

Even as these doubts were creeping in to spoil her pleasure, her ears perked up like Barkley's at the crinkle of his food bag by the hustling and bustling in the hall, and she chuckled at a familiar squabble unfolding in the doorway to the kitchen— Cook barking orders at Ponsonby.

Fortunately, before the bickering grew too acrimonious, the doorbell chimed. The good-natured squabbling ended, and she heard Ponsonby opening the door. After a brief, too quiet conversation at the door, Ponsonby entered the sitting room with the royal dispatch on the finest silver tray she still owned, her late husband's gilded letter opener beside it.

Mary set her needlework down inside her basket before standing. She carefully took the envelope from the tray. Ponsonby's expression was as correct as ever, not even a trace of a smile on his lips, but she knew he was as excited as she was.

She slowly and carefully broke the seal. The tension was palpable, as if the Queen herself was about to spring forth from the envelope. Mary read the dispatch, her eyes moving across the words. She read it a second time, aloud for Ponsonby's benefit. Though she witnessed anticipation gleaming in his eyes, he remained stolid.

To HER GRACE, Mary Elizabeth Culpeper, Duchess of Snodsbury, Greetings.

The Queen requests your service in an important commission for the Crown. You are to be in London by the first of the month to prepare this year's young women for presentation...

WHEN SHE'D FINISHED READING, Ponsonby said, "Would it be appropriate to offer my congratulations, milady? The Queen has chosen wisely."

At the new mention of the Queen, Barkley woke from his slumber and raced out of the room.

"I always felt Barkley understood more than we gave him credit for," Mary said, laughing. "Now I'm sure of it."

But she understood Barkley's mood. With the arrival of this royal summons, all tension dissipated, and relief flooded in until Cook came barging into the room, yelling, "That dog is barking mad. He's doing zoomies across the Axminster carpet."

Mary laughed and then laughed louder before she caught herself with a hand to her lips. A faint smile momentarily illuminated Ponsonby's face, but he, too, quickly regained his composure.

Ignoring the intrusion, Mary replied, "I'm glad you're here,

Cook. I'm sure Ponsonby has informed you of our trip to London?"

"Yes, milady." Cook took off her cap and fiddled with a few loose strands of hair. Her eyes remained trained on the floor.

It wasn't like Cook to be timorous, Mary thought.

"You, of course, will need to accompany us," Mary said. "That won't be a problem?"

Cook's eyes darted up to Mary. "No, milady, no problem at all, and I'm assured I can take what I need, all I need, to do my work properly?"

"You always do your work perfectly, Cook," Mary said, "and you have my assurance, on this occasion, you will not be required to leave anything behind."

Cook cast a puzzled look, an expression as though she was waiting for additional information not previously sprung on her. Then, in one blink of her eye, Cook's demeanor transformed, and she said, "Let's go, Ponsonby. We have work to do." She pulled on Ponsonby as she left the room with the same gusto as she had entered it.

Mary flashed Ponsonby an apologetic smile, though she was truly glad Cook would be bossing *him* around for the next few days and not *her*.

3

CULPEPER HOUSE, LONDON, ENGLAND, MAY 1958

Culpeper House in Knightsbridge, the London home of the Snodsburys, had once been considered one of the finest homes in the capital. Sadly, those days were gone, and the house looked bare on the chilly early May morning when Lady Mary, Ponsonby, Barkley, and Cook arrived to take up residence.

"We must have the old place looking perfect for when the young ladies are here," Lady Mary said to Ponsonby after they'd settled in.

"Having the fires on for a few days will drive away the mustiness," Ponsonby assured. "I believe it's the damp that makes it feel cold."

"It's not just the damp or the mustiness, though, is it? There is emptiness on the walls where pictures once hung. These old dreary curtains," Lady Mary said, gesturing to the faded velvet drapes at the window, "need replacing, and the furniture is threadbare and needs reupholstering." She walked around the room. "The floors need new covers since we sold those beautiful old Persian rugs."

"Not all that can be done in the few days we have," Ponsonby said, "but what can be done will be."

Mary nodded. "See to it," she said firmly.

"Some of the tradespeople may want payment up front," Ponsonby said. "I may have to have furnishings brought from Snodsbury Hall."

"Tell them their wares will be in front of the nation's next generation of stately homemakers," Mary said, "and we're on a commission from the Palace. That should smooth the way." She spoke confidently, but she knew Ponsonby was right. "If that doesn't work, bring things from the country."

"I will do my best, milady," Ponsonby said.

Mary knew in her heart that he'd long since lost confidence in the management of the estate and feared she would be humiliated to find her wishes were no longer enough to have her needs met.

"I do feel for the tradesmen," Lady Mary added. "They have families to feed, where you and I don't. If you can make them understand that this is in their best interests, too, all will be well."

"Yes, milady. Will you be needing anything before I set out on the task?"

"No, thank you," she replied. "I shall telephone the Palace and arrange to meet the social secretary as soon as possible."

"I fear your ladyship will have to change before meeting anyone," Ponsonby said.

Mary looked at her suit. "Bother."

"Yes, milady. Travel by steam train is delightful, and particularly in First Class, but when boarding and disembarking, one is subject to a great deal of soot from the engine."

"I understand some lines are now using diesel locomotives," Mary said, attempting to brush a particularly large piece of soot from her jacket and smearing it down the sleeve. "It can't happen soon enough, I'd say."

"Quite so," Ponsonby said. "Perhaps you'd leave the suit with Cook for cleaning."

Mary sighed. "I fear you're right. I have made that much worse. I'll take your advice and change." She hurried off to her old familiar bedroom.

After changing, Mary was once again fit to be seen in public. She sat in the hall and telephoned the Palace and asked for the social secretary.

"Good afternoon, Lady Mary. I trust you had a pleasant journey?"

"Very pleasant," Mary replied, "and now I'm ready to work. When shall we meet?"

"I will have a pass sent to your home today," Eleanor said. "You're at Culpeper House. Is that correct?"

"I am."

"Wonderful. Just present the pass at the rear entrance to the Palace tomorrow morning at nine," the woman continued. "They will know you're coming and escort you here to my office. Then we can have a good long chat about what's required."

At nine o'clock the following morning, Lady Mary was in the social secretary's office in Buckingham Palace, eager to begin.

"It's so nice to meet you at last, Lady Mary," Eleanor said, shaking Mary's hand.

With Eleanor's hand still in her grasp, Mary said, "I spent much of last night reminiscing about your mother, all my other friends of those days, and the mysteries we solved together." Mary sighed. "I'm afraid I've lost touch with everyone."

"Have a seat," Eleanor said, gesturing.

"Tell me something, Eleanor," Mary said thoughtfully. "Why me? Why didn't you just call on your mother?"

"I did, and Mother recommended you. She said the job needed someone with a special knack, which Mother hasn't got and never had."

Mary stopped herself saying that was true and asked, "Well, why the sudden rush? Did the last person die on the job?" She laughed to show she wasn't being serious.

Eleanor's face grew serious. "Actually, she did."

"Oh, I'm sorry," Mary said. "It must've been very shocking."

Eleanor's expression remained solemn. "That's the other reason Mother thought you would be the best person for this position. I must tell you that the death of Lady Hilary Sinclair, your predecessor, is being investigated. Of course, it won't be found to have anything to do with the Palace."

"Of course but it's no wonder that your mother turned it down," Mary replied.

"Actually, Mother thinks it's murder and was quite excited at the possibility of investigating such," Eleanor said. "That's when she told me of your previous detective skills. Detective Chief Superintendent Griffiths, who Mother says you know from those old days, is the senior man on the case. However, he has his hands full investigating a big jewelry theft. You must have seen it in the newspapers."

"Yes, well, it would be wonderful if the chief superintendent was fully on board." Mary gazed off at a distant memory. "He's the best they have. Even if he can only oversee the investigation, it will make me feel better, though I doubt he'll want us meddling in the case, if there truly is one."

"Wasn't he grateful for the sleuthing assistance? Mother said he was."

"Yes, I suspect he was... when we provided evidence," Mary laughed. "Otherwise, he was either unhappy with our interference or afraid we'd be harmed while collecting the evidence. I fear we were something of a trial to young Inspector Griffiths of the Yard."

Eleanor laughed. "I can see how that would be. If anything happened, he'd be blamed if any harm came to any of you, and by mother's accounts, they were quite serious crimes that you were investigating."

"They were, though we didn't know that at first, which is why we began. If we'd known what we were getting into, we may have been more wary," Mary said, her head tilted in thoughtful recollection. She turned back to spy Eleanor and asked, "But there can't really be murder here, is there?"

"Mother swears there is a long stitch of truth to the rumor that Lady Hilary was murdered."

"Yes, that does sound much like your mother," Mary replied. "Always certain."

Eleanor laughed. "Mother used to embarrass my sister and me when we were young. She would wade into any altercation we encountered, no matter that it wasn't our business, brandishing her handbag like a cudgel. It was humiliating."

"It's admirable," Mary replied. "Championing the underdog, I mean."

Eleanor grimaced. "We saw the inside of more police stations than is good for young ladies, or so we thought at the time anyway."

"I'm surprised with that kind of police record you're employed here." Mary waved her hand.

"Oh, we were never actually involved," Eleanor said with a chuckle. "We were only inside trying to convince the police to let our mother go."

"Tell me more about the details surrounding Lady Hilary's death."

"I really don't know much more, Lady Mary. The details

should be in the police report." Eleanor flashed Mary a coy grin. "As you're familiar with him, he might let you read it."

"He might," Mary said, staring off to a distant memory of yesteryear when she'd last seen the inspector.

"Some of the girls were with Lady Hilary when she died. An unfortunate business."

"That's dreadful. For the girls, I mean, of course," Mary said sympathetically.

"From what I understand," Elanor said, crossing her arms over her desk, "Lady Hilary suffered a seizure and quickly lapsed into a coma during an afternoon tea prior to presenting her lesson plans. She died only a few hours later. The very next day, her plans were to be presented to the Palace."

"Have the plans been approved, or am I to do that as well?" Mary asked.

"They have been approved," Eleanor replied. "All that is required of you is to follow them and be sure the girls are ready for their presentation."

"Surely," Mary said, "they're all young *ladies*? They don't need any *formal* training?"

Eleanor shuffled some papers and smiled. "I don't know how it was when you were presented, Lady Mary," she said, "but when I was presented, we did a series of sessions with courtiers, dance masters, and deportment coaches. It was a bit tedious but fun too."

Mary searched her memories. In truth, she could hardly recall her own presentation.

Finally, she nodded. "I do remember something like that, yes. It was so long ago I can't be sure." Stating this out loud gave her a qualm of doubt. "Shouldn't there be someone who was presented more recently guiding the girls?"

Eleanor laughed. "Believe me, nothing changes with the ball

or the debutantes. If Queen Charlotte herself arrived to attend, she wouldn't find anything amiss."

"Maybe that's why I hear rumors about the ball being ended," Mary queried. "It should have changed."

"The consensus is most people either feel it must remain the same or just be ended," Eleanor replied. "It can't really be *modernized*."

"Then," Mary said, "I feel qualified to carry on with the preparations, but returning to the unfortunate death of my predecessor, why is there so little heard about it in the news?"

"Fortunately for us all, they were out of town when it happened, and the whiff of murder hasn't hit the London papers yet," Eleanor answered. "Also, the newspaper owners have been encouraged to publish very little." She smiled brightly. "Maybe Detective Chief Superintendent Griffiths will commission you to do some investigating while you're working with the new debutantes."

"It doesn't work that way, but I'll have Ponsonby make calls to the chief superintendent upon my return to Culpeper."

Eleanor nodded. "Now to work." She paused. "Shame on me. We launched straight into talking, and I forgot my manners." She stood. "May I offer you a cup of tea, Lady Mary?"

"I'm fine, really. With so much to be done, we should put this investigative business to rest and move on to the details of my service to the Crown."

"Of course, that's why you're here," Eleanor said. "Now, here are the plans Lady Hilary had laid out, with the schedule of classes."

When Eleanor paused, Mary scanned the sheet quickly. "Looks as though Lady Hilary has thought of everything. She must have had previous experience."

Eleanor nodded. "She's prepared the debutantes for the past

five years and has experienced every strange quirk the young women threw at her, and there were many." She smiled. "I have to admit, when Lady Hilary told me of some of the incidents, I remembered experiencing something like them when I was preparing for the ball." Smiling at Mary's quizzical expression, Eleanor said quickly, "Not from me. I mean, they happened when I was preparing. My mother's behavior cured me of ever trying to make a nuisance of *myself*."

Mary laughed. "Your mother was the kindest of souls, if a little too apt to become carried away by her feelings."

Eleanor nodded, a fond smile on her face.

"I'll read the plans in detail, and if I have questions, I'll telephone you later, if I may?"

"Of course. I'll be in my office until five, but there's something you need to be aware of."

"Something serious?" Mary asked.

"It shouldn't be, but it does make this ball a little more than just a beautiful social event."

"Now I'm worried," Mary said.

Eleanor laughed. "You needn't be. I've no doubt anything will occur to make you so. It's just that, this year, we have a princess in attendance."

"Why?"

"The King of Tzatzikistan, Raheem the Second, has recently moved away from his country's alliance with the Eastern Bloc and is negotiating an alliance with us and the other Western nations. It's his daughter who will be in attendance."

"An old-fashioned way of making friends," Mary said, "using a daughter, a princess, as the inducement. Does he hope for a marriage with one of our Princes?"

"I can't say what the diplomatic maneuverings will be," Eleanor replied carefully, "only that the princess is to be introduced to our Royal Family and Society. The ball is her 'coming out' in both the social and the diplomatic worlds, if you like."

"Does the girl have any training or background that would help her in this new role?" Mary continued before Eleanor could answer, "Isn't Tzatzikistan a Muslim country and, until recently, a Communist one?"

"Up until the recent counter-revolution, it's true they looked to the East for their society, but Raheem has recently recovered the lands his father ruled and thrown out the Communists."

"Still, that was only months ago," Mary said. "The girl can't have learned anything about our ways during her childhood."

"Actually, she grew up in the West during Raheem's exile, and she has come to us directly from a finishing school in Geneva. You'll find she is perfectly accustomed to our ways."

"Does she speak English?"

"She does and speaks it as well as you or I," Eleanor said.

"Will there be any special requirements?" Mary asked.

"Only that she will be closely guarded by her own people on her journeys to and from your home and there will be guards from our Special Services near the house while she is there," Eleanor assured Mary. "They are supposed to be invisible, so you may not even notice them."

Mary frowned. When she was sleuthing before the War, her experience with guards was that they were consequently quite easy to spot based on their size and fitness.

"Very well," Mary said. "Now, if I may, I'd like to return to the death of Lady Hilary. Has there been any explanation of why she became ill and died? Any medical explanation, I mean?"

"None that I've heard," Eleanor said. "It is all very hush-hush."

"I don't like that. Something isn't right."

"That's why my mother says it's murder, and the girls do too," Eleanor added.

"What did the authorities identify or notice at the time?"

"They were taking afternoon tea when Lady Hilary appeared to be about to sneeze. She brought her silk scarf to her nose to stop the sneeze. She held it to her nose for a moment, breathing deeply, appeared to have a seizure, and then passed out. Help was sought quickly, but they couldn't rouse her, and an ambulance was sent for. She never regained consciousness and died in the hospital that same evening."

"The scarf was recovered, I assume?"

"It wasn't immediately thought of as the *problem*," Eleanor said, "and when the police arrived the following morning, no one knew where it was, so no, it wasn't found."

"It wasn't with Lady Hilary?"

"No, and it wasn't in the ambulance," Eleanor said, "because the police searched after her death when they were brought in to investigate."

"Why would she use her scarf and not a handkerchief?" Mary wondered aloud.

"The girls say she couldn't find her handkerchief and her scarf was at hand," Eleanor replied.

"What did the inquest say?"

"Death by causes unknown. It's still open while the police continue their inquiries. Again, Detective Chief Superintendent Griffiths will give you better information on this than I can."

Mary nodded. "I hope so."

"But it can have nothing to do with the ball, Lady Mary. We're all sure of that."

"And I'm sure you're right," Mary said more confidently than she felt.

Sudden death was always disturbing though often entirely innocent.

What was equally disturbing was the knowledge Ivor Griffiths, then inspector and now detective chief superintendent, and she were to meet again. Theirs had been a strange relationship, constantly bickering, often antagonistic, but his concern for her she never doubted.

4

SUSPICIOUS CIRCUMSTANCES

Returning to Culpeper House from her meeting with the secretary in the car which had traveled with them to London via train, Mary sketched a mental list of the preparations while she observed the passing motorists bustling through the city streets.

"Ponsonby, you'll need to ring our old friend, Detective Chief Superintendent Griffiths, when we return."

"Yes, of course, milady. Shall I say what it is about?"

Lady Mary recounted her conversation with the office secretary.

Ponsonby pursed his lips in the rearview mirror. "Is it wise to become involved in such matters, milady, when you already have so much to do?"

"I'm sure it's nothing for us to be concerned about, but I feel it will be nice to rekindle the old friendship with the good chief superintendent, and it can't hurt to have another friend while we're in the city," Mary said.

Ponsonby coughed discreetly, in the way Mary knew he had doubts about her proposal.

"Should we *not* contact the chief superintendent?" she asked.

"Well, milady," Ponsonby drawled, "I recall you telling me that the last time you saw Inspector Griffiths, he made it known that he never wanted to encounter you or any of your sister sleuths again."

"Well, we weren't exactly right with our solution that last time, and it caused him a bit of trouble with his superiors," Mary explained, "but clearly it hasn't held him back because he's now a *chief superintendent*, so I'm sure he'll have forgiven, if not forgotten, all that by now."

"Very well, milady," Ponsonby replied, though his tone was flat.

"He will be very pleased to hear from us," Mary said firmly.

Ponsonby was too busy pulling the car up to Culpeper House to reply.

The house was a stately two-story stone building that once bustled with grand parties and the laughter of fine friends. A shell—old and tired much as Mary herself did.

"I shall change out of my good tweed before I work on the place," Mary said with a pensive expression on her face.

Minus the luxurious draperies, the large sashed windows appeared empty and drab from the outside. That song, *This Old House*, popular a few years before, sprang readily to mind as she remembered happier days in residence.

"Summon Cook for me first, please."

"Yes, of course, milady," Ponsonby said.

"Is that a smile I see, Ponsonby?"

"Apologies, milady. You have found me out. I am sure you will be pleased by the progress this afternoon."

A delivery truck pulled around from the back and passed by the car, and they both glanced in the direction of the driveway.

"Looks as though things are coming along," Mary suggested.

"Of course, milady."

"Well, let's move inside and inspect the work, shall we?"

Ponsonby left the hall to carry out his instructions from Lady Mary regarding lunch and re-establish their link to DCS Griffiths. The timing was fortuitous, for the chief superintendent was in his office and, he said, happy to renew acquaintances with the duchess. The two men briefly reminisced about old times before Ponsonby brought Mary to the telephone.

"Detective Chief Superintendent," Mary said, "congratulations on your new title."

"Thank you, Your Grace," Griffiths said, laughing, "but it's some years since it happened. I quite forget there was a time when I was just an ordinary inspector."

They, too, discussed old times before Mary said, "I didn't just telephone for the very real pleasure of talking with you again. I also rang to ask for your help."

"What kind of help?"

Mary explained about her new role, how she came to be in it, and, in particular, why she wanted to know more about the death of her predecessor.

"I'm aware of that death," Griffiths said. "At present, it doesn't appear to be suspicious. It appears quite accidental."

"If that is so," Mary replied, "I will be extremely relieved. I don't want to discover I'm next to die in a plot against the monarchy or the debutante ball."

Griffiths laughed. "You may be overreacting, Your Grace. There's no suggestion of anything like that, and the Special Branch people have investigated the matter."

"I've heard rumors the debutante ball is not as popular as in past times," Mary stated.

"Yes, but mainly it's unpopular with the Palace and the others in that set. They think it no longer fits the image of a modern business-like monarchy." Griffiths' voice chimed as he continued, "When the Palace wants to end it, they will end it, but it won't be by killing the ball's social director, I assure you."

"So the police are happy to conclude she died of natural causes?" Mary asked.

"I didn't say that," Griffiths replied carefully. "It's likely she inhaled something poisonous, possibly from her silk scarf. At least, that's what the forensic experts say, but we don't have the scarf, so their guess is as good as yours or mine."

"My guess would be if the scarf is missing, it's how the poison was administered," Mary said.

"But we don't really know she was poisoned," Griffiths said. "There were traces of strychnine in her body, certainly, but not enough to kill someone who was in good health."

"Then can they really be sure it did kill her?" Mary questioned.

"It's why they are struggling to give better information," Griffiths said then added sarcastically, "though, in my experience, they're hesitant to give a clear answer at *any* time."

"You said 'someone in good health,' Chief Superintendent."

"Lady Hilary, sadly, *wasn't* in good health, and it's possible that made it lethal. I can't say more than that because tests and analysis are still in progress."

"Then she was likely poisoned?" Mary urged.

"Possibly, but it could equally likely have been entirely accidental," Griffiths said. "The scarf may have been exposed to strychnine in some way, rather than being deliberately impregnated with it. That's the way the experts are leaning, anyway. All I'm really saying is do not worry for your own safety."

Mary considered his words carefully. From an outsider's viewpoint, the likelihood of it being a deliberate murder was low, but she wasn't an outsider any longer, and she might be next.

She thanked him, and they ended the call.

MARY AWOKE the next morning to the unfamiliar noises of workmen and the din of London traffic. She was too accustomed to the country quiet of Snodsbury. Even though the house was set well back from the street, she was keenly aware of the racket around her. Buses and lorries rumbled by, taxis accelerated as they weaved between the bigger vehicles, milk bottles clinked on carts, and commuters chattered loudly as they rushed to the nearest tube station.

Her need to be outside as much as possible during the warm months spurred her to dress quickly. Once clothed, she made her way downstairs where Ponsonby was drawing back the drapes and Cook was busy in the kitchen, judging by the clatter of pans.

"Good morning, milady," Ponsonby said, walking ahead to unlock the terrace doors for her.

"It's a beautiful morning," Mary agreed. "I shall be in the garden when Cook has breakfast ready. Come, Barkley."

Ponsonby followed her out of the doors and Mary settled on a bench nearby. "I'd like to speak to DCS Griffiths as soon as I can," she said.

Ponsonby took out his pocket watch, checked the time, and said, "I fancy the detective chief superintendent will be in his office. I'll telephone him immediately."

Mary barely had time enough to enjoy the dewy flowers before Ponsonby arrived again to say he had Griffiths on the phone.

"Detective Chief Superintendent, good morning," Mary began when she picked up the handset. "Has there been any news concerning Lady Hilary's death?"

She heard him chuckle. "Good morning," he said. "Is that keeping you awake?"

"I can't sleep because of London's noise," Mary replied, "which gives me lots of time to think. You will tell me immediately if the police decide it likely Lady Hilary was murdered, won't you?"

"I certainly will, Your Grace, but I don't expect there to be a change overnight," Griffiths replied. "They still think it's an accidental death, but if it isn't, and it has a link to the ball, you'll be provided protection."

"I have more questions. Did Lady Hilary have any obvious enemies?"

"None. She was a mild, rather old-fashioned lady who kept to herself, save for her royal duties," Griffiths said.

"Would there be any other reason to stop the ball?"

"Your appointment is proof against that. Killing her didn't stop it."

"Very well," Mary said. "Unless there's anything else, I shall accept the official view for now."

The inspector hesitated before answering, "Nothing else. That I know of."

"Are you wavering, Chief Superintendent? Or am I reading too much into your choice of words?"

"I have no reason to disbelieve the evidence, and analysis, the officers and lab staff have gathered and presented," Griffiths said. "It just doesn't feel right to me, and that's the truth of it."

"Thank you for being honest with me, Chief Superintendent," Mary said. "My instinct also says this was unlikely to be an accidental death."

"You don't have any known medical conditions, do you?" Griffiths asked.

"None," Mary replied. "I'm safe from that kind of accident. Why it should be about Queen Charlotte's Ball, I can't imagine, so I'm safe there too. Lady Hilary had no other facets to her life that might warrant this kind of murderous response if it was deliberate?"

"She did not," Griffiths answered. "The ball was the only controversial issue in her life and its controversial-ness, if there's such a word, is so small as to be unbelievable as a motive."

"Then I'm sorry to have disturbed your work, Chief Superintendent," Mary said, ending the call.

From everything she'd just heard, the police were losing interest in Lady Hilary's death, and she had no choice but to look out for herself.

Mary opened a small diary she'd brought with her. In it were the numbers of three of her old friends, sister sleuths from the nineteen-thirties. She dialed each of the numbers and asked to speak to her friends respectively. In each case, after catching up on their lives and her own, she gave the same speech.

"I'm calling because I want your help but not directly."

This was greeted by disappointed groans from each.

"Your daughters are in my debutante classes, and I'd like them to keep their eyes and ears open among the group."

"They're too young to be sleuthing," was the general answer from the mothers, to which Mary replied by reminding them they'd been their daughters' age during their first investigations together. This was reluctantly accepted, though there was a general belief they'd been a lot more mature than their daughters were, which Mary ignored. In Mary's opinion, she and her friends had been equally immature and inexperienced all those years ago.

"If you're agreeable, I'd like to invite your daughters to meet me in the morning and let them decide if they want to assist," Mary said.

The mothers finally agreed after their initial hesitations, and Mary finished her speech, saying, "Don't tell them we've talked.

I'd like them to decide for themselves. This can only be if they willingly want to take part."

Mary then telephoned the houses once more, asking to speak to the daughters this time. Each young lady accepted her invitation to a meeting at Culpeper House on the following day. As she finished each call, she began to wonder if the youngsters were right for the job.

5

RECRUITED

Ponsonby entered the morning room the following day with his serious, squared butler-face on, and Mary knew her guests had arrived.

"The young ladies, Lady Mary," Ponsonby said, standing aside to allow them to enter. "The Honorable Margery Marmalade, The Honorable Winnefred Winters, and The Honorable Dorothy Dillyard."

Mary rose and smiled at them, holding out her hands to greet them. "I recognize your mothers in each of you," she remarked, smiling. "I hope you won't mind me saying that."

She was assured they didn't mind as each young woman took a seat offered.

"Tell Cook we're ready for tea," Mary directed to Ponsonby, dismissing him as she took her carefully chosen seat so she could observe each of the young debs as they talked. "First, I want to know more about you and how your mothers are, of course. I haven't been in Society for quite some time. I feel I'm out of touch." Mary relaxed her posture for the casual conversation. "Do you all know each other?"

Each nodded, assuring Lady Mary that they did.

"Perhaps you can start, Lady Margery?" Mary offered.

"You can call me Margie, milady," Margery replied.

Without waiting to be asked, Winnefred said, "And I prefer Winnie, with an 'IE', please and thank you."

Lady Mary looked to the third young lady. "And you?"

"Dotty, thank you, milady. I don't really care for the name, but I've always been called that, and I'm used to it now."

"I'll do that. Now, tell me, how well do you know each other?"

"Since boarding school," Winnie responded matter-of-factly.

"And we're all going to the same college now, Girton College, Cambridge, so we can earn a degree at the end of our study," Dotty interjected.

"Your knowing each other is good news," Mary said, "because I was hoping you three could be my helpers, and to do what I have in mind, you'll need to trust one another, which is much easier to do when you're already well acquainted."

"In what way do you want our help?" Margie asked. Waves of honeysuckle-colored hair swayed past her ears as she leaned forward in her seat and placed her hands on her knees.

"Is it about detecting?" Dotty asked eagerly, her frizzy ginger curls spiraled out from her head in every direction. "When I was young, mother told me about your adventures sleuthing."

"If it's detecting, I'm in," Winnie interjected. "My mother also told me of the adventures you had together, and I won't be found wanting when my time comes." Her short, straight black hair moved like a curtain with her head, a physical expression of her strongest character trait.

Margie giggled. "That's why I asked. If it's detecting, count me in too. If it's looking after spoiled debs and keeping them in line, then no thank you! I won't be a dorm room monitor. That's a job for her." She pointed a short chubby finger at Winnie, who protested with a scowl.

Mary smiled. "I'm glad your mothers have regaled you with stories of the olden days and you're ready to follow in their footsteps. I want to be certain they explained things factually and that they didn't give you the child's version. Sleuthing often involves a great deal of discomfort, dirt, and danger."

"Dirty dirt? Like mud?" Margie asked with her nose snubbed up.

Mary exerted a calming smile at the bouncy young lady vibrating in her seat. Margie was going to need work, not only on her facial expressions but also her jerky movements, before being presented at court.

The girls nodded while Mary gently fanned herself.

Mary continued in a serious tone, "Real danger, not the sort where you cross your fingers or click your heels and you're alive again."

"Deathly danger?" Margie asked.

"Yes, deathly danger," Mary agreed. "Now, are you still in?"

This time, their responses were slower coming. Mary eyed each of the girls. Winnie Winters jutted her chin and arched her back, while Dotty's blank expression left Mary wondering about her true personality.

"I had an older brother killed in Kenya," Margie replied, slouching back into the wing back chair across from Lady Mary. "It would be hard for my parents if anything happened to me." She paused before picking her head back up, her voice less timid. "But I have another older and a younger brother and a sister so they wouldn't be left alone."

Mary eyed the young lady as she worked through her decision.

Margie's stout body positioned straighter, and her eyes serious, she said, "I'm still in."

"I'm not an only child either," Winnie said in a monotone voice. "Mother will understand."

"Same for me," Dotty added. "If our mothers had wanted us to be shrinking violets, they wouldn't have told us tales of their own derring-do."

Ponsonby and Cook entered the room, bringing tea and a tiered cake stand of pastries, which brought an end to the conversation for a moment.

"Thank you, Cook."

Cook, who was still unfamiliar to serving, curtsied stiffly and left as Mary prepared to pour the tea. Ponsonby was about to follow her out of the door when Mary called him back.

"Ponsonby," she said, "meet our new sleuthing assistants. Ladies, meet Ponsonby who, your mothers may have told you, is the master of all things technical in criminal investigations. He dusts for fingerprints, performs chemical analysis, photographs crime scenes, opens doors that are locked, and scales heights sensible people won't."

Winnie gazed at Ponsonby with a disbelieving expression while Dotty fiddled with the leaves of a plant beside her seat avoiding eye contact with anyone else.

Lady Mary smiled. "You will need to learn to look beyond the descriptors of young or old," she said. "We understand your surprise, but after all, Ponsonby and I were also once young."

To emphasize her point, Mary snapped her fan shut, and Dotty jumped in her seat, as leaves from the plant she'd been tugging at fell to the floor.

"We haven't lost our abilities just because our hair is now white," Lady Mary said, plumping her hair, "as you will learn in the coming days."

Embarrassment showed on Margie's soft pink skin. "I'm sure I speak for all three of us when I say we have no disparaging thoughts about *older* people."

Dotty nodded like a bobblehead toy.

Mary dismissed the notion with a wave of her fan. "Now,"

she said, "Ponsonby, will you and Cook ensure lunch will be prompt? I want to learn all about these young ladies before the others arrive for our first class."

AFTER LUNCH, the old-fashioned door chime set Mary's teeth on edge. Not for the first time, she decided to have it replaced very soon. The young women were finally arriving. She steadied herself in preparation to greet them.

Mary and her new assistants stayed where they were and listened as Ponsonby welcomed the new arrivals. Cook led the young women to the ballroom where the classes were to be held.

Minutes later, Ponsonby entered the morning room to announce the whole class was assembled. He noted to Lady Mary, "Forty-seven in total, milady, and with our three assistants, that makes fifty."

"If the names match the list, we're ready to begin."

"Yes, milady. Each of the ladies that arrived is on the Palace's list."

"And I see, Barkley's going to guard them in the ballroom." She nodded to the retreating rump of her regal corgi.

Ponsonby gave the slightest of smiles as he looked through the open door to spy the corgi passing by.

Mary rose to her feet, and all three walked through the hall and into the ballroom. As she entered, Mary looked about. She was pleased to note that the workers had indeed brought the room up to ducal standards, the perfect place to entertain the young debutantes, lovely in every detail. The wooden floor was once again polished for dancing. The cleaned, velvet drapes framing the tall windows glowed in the family colors of scarlet fringed with golden tassels. The room smelled slightly of fresh paint, but it was worth it to have the walls freshened up. The ceiling, with its trompe-l'oeil scenes of the family's history up until the turn of the century, raised the spirit of the room and almost brought a tear to her eye. To be part of this ancient lineage was indeed something to be witnessed.

She gazed down the length of the room. The fifty young ladies would be coupled with young gentlemen, introduced later, and practice would take place in this splendid ballroom designed to accommodate hundreds of guests.

Mentally shaking herself, Mary moved her eyes from the room to her pupils. She walked toward the now silent group and looked at a slim, raven-haired woman who was viewing her with a cold eye.

Ponsonby made the introductions. "Princess Jezebel, Your Grace."

"Welcome, Princess," Mary said, extending her hand. "I hope you're finding everything to your satisfaction in your London stay?"

"My father has been very careful to ensure that I am," the princess replied then nodded dismissively.

Lady Mary hid her own reaction.

After the princess moved away, Ponsonby muttered, "Not proper. Not proper at all."

Barkley followed behind the princess as she made her way farther into the ballroom.

"Shall we, milady?" Ponsonby gestured as he led her to meet each of the girls.

Most of the young ladies knew many of the others in the room and had already joined up in small convivial groups talking excitedly about anything and everything. A few appeared to know no one, Princess Jezebel being the most obvious example. Her cold, haughty manner, Mary thought, might just be due to being dropped in a room of fifty people she didn't know.

Finally, Mary had met everyone and took up a place at the end of the room, calling them all to order. "Ladies, today is very much a meet-and-greet day, and I have some small ice-breaking activities to start us off." She outlined the first activity. When the girls had begun mingling, she turned to Ponsonby and whispered, "I fear we might have bitten off more than we can chew, my old friend."

"Your Grace will soon have them eating out of your hand."

Mary laughed. "Horses are easier to bribe. These fillies will need more than sugar lumps or carrots."

6

BARKLEY TO THE RESCUE

Mary shook her head to clear her thoughts and quickly brought the students to attention with a sharp clap of her hands. "Ladies, I'll have your attention please. This morning, and all the days between now and the ball, we're going to cover the basics, the three Ds—deportment, discipline, and, of course, dancing. I know you are all finished young ladies, but this ball will launch you into society as no other can. These next few weeks spent together are your opportunity to be sure you don't set off on the wrong foot."

As she was speaking, Mary was happy that most of the young ladies stood composed and ready for instruction. All of them had attended fine finishing schools and would know what was expected. Nevertheless, Mary knew she could leave nothing to chance. They all had to reach a level of accomplishment suitable for meeting royalty in the way of the previous century.

Barkley sat stoically beside her, his head moving from person to person, sizing up the crowd, as Lady Mary spoke. She was amused by the similarities of pampered pets to pampered children–and their excited fits of wild activity. Such behavior must be restrained.

Mary worried that the princess was not versed in any of the three Ds. Eleanor had said the girl was perfectly trained, but Mary's first meeting with the princess hadn't been encouraging.

At the break, Mary called Margie to her side. "I'd like you to befriend the princess and assist her."

"Yes, milady. Shall I gather important clues?"

"Just be welcoming," Mary replied, smiling. "Do keep your eyes and ears open."

"Oh," Margie asked. "Is this who we're investigating?"

"No," Mary replied quickly. "The princess doesn't know anyone here and needs a friend. That's all."

Margie appeared disappointed, but she assured Mary she would introduce the princess to the others.

After letting Margie spend some minutes with Jezebel, Mary once again caught the group's attention and resumed their lessons. She had more assignments in store for her sleuthing understudies, but those she would share with them after the day's classes had ended.

As the students walked through the different exercises, Mary made her way around the room, adjusting postures, correcting positions, and dissuading fidgeting before announcing another break. She surveyed the scene as the girls descended on the tables of snacks and tea and sighed. Mary caught Winnie Winter's eye and signaled her to her side.

"Winnie, I would like you to befriend the princess. The Honorable Margie has misunderstood her assignment." Mary shot a pointed look at Margie, who was piling a plate of snacks from the buffet, and then to the princess, who was standing alone, scowling. "I asked her to help Jezebel meet new friends, not leave her alone in a corner the moment the snacks came out."

Winnie, following Mary's gaze, grinned at the sight. She

nodded then added, "I'm not famous for tact, you know, but I'll do my best."

Originally, Mary had chosen Margie because she'd thought Dotty too scatterbrained and Winnie too brusque. Now, she'd discovered Margie was easily distracted and thought brusque was the next best option.

"Then, once you've made your introductions, find a suitable excuse to bring her to me. Between us, we can set her at ease."

As Mary's eyes followed Winnie crossing the floor to the princess, she wondered if Winnie would guess it was also intended to be a learning opportunity for the young sleuth.

The princess didn't show any anger at being singled out, which suggested Winnie must have had more tact than she'd given herself credit for. After a moment, Winnie and Jezebel came to Mary's side.

"Princess Jezebel," Lady Mary greeted her, "I hope you'll make friends quickly. Are you acquainted with any of the young women here?"

The princess shook her head. "No. I went to school in Switzerland, but my father is keen to have closer ties with this country, so here I am."

"Some of the girls went to finishing school in Switzerland," Mary said. "Maybe you'll find someone you know sooner than you think."

"Unlikely," the princess said haughtily. "I went to a very exclusive school only for royalty."

"Then we shall have to make sure you meet lots of new friends in this class so you won't be sitting on your own in your hotel throughout your visit," Mary said. "If you're to forge links, we will do our best to make that happen."

"I'm not staying in a hotel," Jezebel said. "I'm staying at the embassy. My father thought it was safer."

"I'm sure he knows best," Mary replied. "Still, I hope you'll make enough friends to be happy while you're here in London. Your stay shouldn't be all about diplomacy. That would be extremely dull."

"I've only been here two days," Jezebel said, "and it is already dull."

Winnie's eyes widened at Jezebel's improper comment.

"Then these classes will have a second purpose for you," Mary replied doggedly, "and perhaps friendship will be the more important one."

Jezebel's lazy expression suggested she didn't agree, but she remained silent.

"Now that the rush is over," Mary said brightly, "you must help yourself to something from the table. My cook will be tickled pink to know she's been serving a real-life princess."

* . * . * . 🐾 . * . * . * . *

"IS EVERYTHING TO YOUR SATISFACTION, MILADY?" Ponsonby asked after all the girls had gone.

"Yes, but I'm in need of some air," Mary said with a relieved sigh. "I'm not used to such excitement. It's been a long time..." She paused. "I'll take Barkley out onto the terrace."

"It's a warm spring afternoon, and the sun is out. May I suggest the nearby park? The trees are covered in blossoms today, and you know how much His Royal Highness Barkley enjoys chasing the squirrels." Ponsonby flashed a smile at the dog perched beside his own mistress.

"We really shouldn't encourage that behavior."

"Barkley knows when to practice *his* three Ds. You needn't be concerned."

Barkley let out a commanding "woof" of confirmation.

Mary smiled. Ponsonby wasn't wrong, but she looked sternly at Barkley. "No chasing the squirrels. Do you hear?"

Barkley assumed an outraged demeanor of a greatly wronged dog. Besides, no well-born dog would chase squirrels.

Ponsonby winked at Barkley. "Fine dog. A fine dog indeed."

Mary, suitably dressed, and Barkley left the house and set off at a brisk pace to the park. Unbuttoning her overcoat in the warmth of the sun, Mary took a deep breath. "No pea-soupers today, Barkley, as the papers would say. The Clean Air Act appears to be working. I look forward to the day when those horrible fogs are gone forever."

Barkley sniffed the air before herding a trail of stray leaves blowing down the path just ahead of Mary.

"The young ladies were a bit skittish in class. What do you make of their levels of attention, Barkley?" Mary asked as he captured one bit of the errant foliage and barked it into submission. "They were just nervous, I suspect. I recognize great potential in a handful of these girls," she murmured to herself.

They entered the park. Blackbirds with their melodious songs and, surprising to Mary, a pair of Kestrels were busy tending to their young. All was quiet save for the parents' calls and the tiny chirps of newborn chicks. The afternoon was still too early for those who had an occupation and too late for the nannies with prams, who would be settling the children for their evening meal before reacquainting them with their parents.

The warm sun and the distant hum of traffic were oddly soothing after her afternoon of accomplishments. The young ladies were, of course, ladies and not really a handful, but shepherding fifty young people through various scenes in a way they wouldn't find condescending drained her energy.

The obvious ways—beloved of governesses everywhere, like walking with a book on your head or correctly serving tea—

wouldn't do. She needed to be more clever, or she would lose their confidence. Lady Hilary's plans included the "what" but not the "how." Meanwhile, Mary thought the park's landscaped masses of tulips would soothe her agitated spirits, but before she knew it, her tension returned to her worries over Snodsbury.

Marking his territory as they walked, Barkley's main concern was none other than the elusive squirrel, so he stayed on high alert growling at the fluffy-tailed menaces that scampered over the walkway.

Mary sighed. "Barkley, I said no squirrels," she said just as a small gray fluffball stopped on the path to nibble on a seed. The catkins of the London Plane trees were vanishing with the spring, being replaced by a thick, green cover overhead.

His ears forward, Barkley gave Mary a severe glare that said, without any mistake, her lack of resolution on the squirrel matter would lose them both the respect of the creatures in this park. Mary remained unmoved by his silent rebuke, and they continued to a corner of the path where rhododendrons grew heartily on both sides. Barkley's growl increased in intensity.

"I don't care how many squirrels are in there, Barkley," Mary stated. "You're not chasing them."

Mary paused and listened intently. Her sense of hearing was perfect, yet she wasn't picking up on any of the noises that her big-dog-on-little-legs was.

Hackles raised, his tail bristled and stiff, Barkley growled at the shrubbery, backing away a few steps.

Mary stopped and eyed the bushes cautiously. "What is it, Barkley?"

She stared at him, his legs stiff and nose wrinkled in alarm.

"What's this defensive behavior, Barkley?" Mary asked, puzzled. "I don't see anything. Do you smell something?"

Unable or unwilling to move, Barkley continued facing the bushes, growling.

"Is someone in there?" Mary called, nervously.

They would look silly running away from a gardener, she thought. She glanced around the small park, hoping to see other people, but no one was in sight and not a soul to be heard. Surely, if someone was in the bushes, she would hear rustling against branches or treading on last year's fallen leaves?

"Oh, come on, Barkley," she said at last, tugging at his leash. "Your nose is leading you astray. What is worrisome in Norfolk is everyday stuff here in London."

She stepped forward, and Barkley forged ahead of her, taking the lead.

As the path narrowed between a patch of over-growing bushes, a man leapt out, a knife raised in his right hand, aimed straight toward Mary's heart. Before the man could make a move, Barkley pounced and bit his sharp teeth into the man's calf.

Instinctively, Mary raised her handbag up as a shield as the man's hand swung down. The assailant's knife punctured the padded, quilted leather and lodged itself in the bag's contents as Mary wrestled herself away.

"Help!" Mary screamed.

She tried using the bag as leverage to wrest the knife from his grip. For a moment, the man's free hand grabbed at her throat. She twisted to get away, and he snagged his arm on the knife while they struggled. Barkley's continued attack had the man kicking to shake him off. Before the assault could continue further, Mary heard a police whistle. Whipping his head around, still shaking his leg and arm, the attacker searched for his escape while Mary and Barkley tried desperately to hang on until help arrived.

The pair almost succeeded in taking down the assailant, but they were overpowered. His actions desperate, he finally shook them both off and ran while Mary clung tightly to the leash with Barkley tugging fiercely, trying to give chase.

Barkley returned to Mary's side with a triumphant grin. A small piece of the man's pant leg hung from his teeth.

One constable arrived and then another. The first asked, "Are you all right, madam?"

"I am," Mary said. She held up her mutilated bag with the knife still stuck in it. "You might pull some fingerprints off this."

The man extricated the knife and wrapped it in a bag.

"Did he wear gloves?" the second constable asked.

"Oh, yes," Mary replied. "He did and a balaclava that covered his whole face except his eyes. They were dark brownish."

"Perhaps you could give us some details now while it is fresh in your mind. A detective can call on you tomorrow for anything you might remember later." He opened his notebook and waited with a stubby pencil in hand for her to speak.

Barkley tugged on the leash.

"Shouldn't one of you be following the man?" Mary asked, echoing Barkley's urgency.

"He'll be long gone by now, ma'am. Now, did you recognize him at all?"

Mary sighed and resigned herself to answering their questions.

When she was finished, he said, "Thank you, ma'am. This will help us catch him. I expect he was after your jewels."

"I've just told you," Mary cried in frustration. "He lunged at me with a knife. He didn't threaten me with it, nor did he demand I hand over my jewels, or purse for that matter."

"I imagine that was because he stumbled when your dog bit him," the policeman replied. "We don't have knife attacks here in this part of the city."

"You do now," Mary said, almost shouting. Really, this was

beyond a parody of policing. "This was an attack, not a robbery. My dog bit him *after* he tried to stab me to death!"

Growing increasingly agitated, the bobby's tone clipped Mary's nerves. "Why would anyone want to kill you, madam?"

Mary paused, considering if she should mention her new role and employment with the Palace or what happened to the woman who held it before. She bit into her tongue, realizing all that would be perceived as ludicrous. She resigned herself to speak to DCS Griffiths the instant she got home.

"Never mind," Mary said crossly. "Would it be too much to ask one of you to escort me back to my residence?" She paused, taking measure of the apathetic look on the man's face. "In case the culprit is hiding somewhere along my return journey?" she added.

"Certainly, madam," the man replied. "I'll do that." He stepped aside and waved her forward.

BACK AT CULPEPER HOUSE, Mary's frazzled nerves were jangled again when Cook learned that Mary had been attacked. She ascended from her usual domain of the kitchen to give Lady Mary a piece of her mind.

From the long, jumbled lecture she got as Cook helped her off with her coat, Mary couldn't quite be sure whether it was her being late for dinner or the attack that disturbed her outraged retainer the most.

After a moment, when Cook paused for breath, Mary placed her hand on her arm and said, "Cook, I'm quite whole, see?" She turned in a slow circle to demonstrate her health and vigor.

"That's very well, milady," Cook said, not in the least molli-fied, "but if you're going to be fighting off assassins again, you can't do that when you haven't eaten properly. You'll sicken and die, and that's a fact. Now you sit down and eat!"

Seeing that the elderly woman was genuinely frightened, Mary conceded, "You're quite right, Cook. I should take more care. I can't face anything heavy. It was quite a shock, but if you'll bring some of your excellent syllabub, I promise to eat every bit of it." She smiled and gripped Cook's arm, and Cook, in turn, covered Mary's hand with a clammy hand of arthritic fingers.

THE FOLLOWING MORNING, Mary was again reminded that what had happened to her affected others when she answered a telephone call from the chief superintendent.

"I'm perfectly well, Chief Superintendent," Mary said in answer to his brusque question concerning her health.

"I'm aware you weren't physically injured," he replied. "The report I read this morning said as much. I was concerned for your well-being as much as your person."

"I'm fine. We're both fine," Mary said, chuckling.

"We're going to need to allocate protection for you during the rest of this commission you've taken on."

"You'll do no such thing," Mary cried indignantly. "I'm perfectly capable of looking after myself, thank you."

"You were lucky this time," Griffiths said bluntly. "You may not be next time."

As this was what Mary had been thinking only the night before, she found it hard to dismiss his concern.

"Chief Superintendent," she said at last, "your concern is much appreciated, but there's no reason to believe that this attack was anything to do with my commission. It may just have been a poor deranged criminal."

Griffiths was silent for a moment, considering her response. Then, he said, "Very well, Your Grace, but if there's even a hint of trouble in the next few days, you will have an officer with you whenever you leave the house."

"I'm sure there'll be no need for anything so drastic," she said, "but you see now that my suspicions about Lady Hilary's death may not be entirely misplaced?"

"You're convincing me all over again that I should detail a man to escort you, Your Grace."

Mary laughed. "Then I'll say no more. Thank you for your concern, Chief Superintendent, but I must go and prepare for the next volley of classes."

STILL SMILING at the inspector's anxiety for her safety, Mary awaited the arrival of the young debutantes in the large ball-room of Culpeper House. The polished brass and newly cleaned curtains breathed elegant nostalgia into the room. This time, the ladies assembled in dazzling evening gowns, not presentation gowns of course. These gowns had seen the pleasure of a ball or outing several times over already. Indeed, she heard whispered comments about some dresses having been worn *too often*.

Mary shook her head at such childishness while she gazed around the room and sighed. Fond memories of balls in her own past, in this very room, flashing vividly through her mind, days gone by when her husband was still alive and the house formed a significant part of London Society, when she and the world were so much younger. She sighed a deep sigh and resigned herself to the task at hand.

Just ahead, Mary noticed Winnie, Margie, and Dotty

exchange glances. Perhaps hearing Mary's exaggerated sigh, they flitted to her side.

Winnie commented, "I recognize that from my own mother whenever she reminisces, especially when we attend events."

"It's nothing to trouble yourselves over." Mary paused to take their measure. "What do you make of our princess, ladies?"

For a moment, the girls were quiet. Winnie turned to shoot a pointed stare at Jezebel.

Then, Margie replied, "I thought people from the Middle East dressed in their more traditional wardrobes?"

Dotty nodded as her fingers danced in the air as if to choreograph an imaginary symphony.

Winnie said, "I expect she doesn't because she went to school in Switzerland and bought western fashions."

"Why did she go to school in Switzerland if her father is such a friend of ours? I'd like to know." Dotty finally joined the conversation.

"Maybe her father didn't like *his* English school and wanted something less strict for his children," Mary replied. "Or maybe he has only recently come around to seeing our country as a friend. After all, Switzerland won't come to his aid if another revolution happens."

Margie nodded. "I expect you're right. Yes." She nodded, a firm gesture. "Jezebel isn't very princess-like because of her continental schooling."

"How did you form this opinion?" Mary asked, puzzled.

"The way she talks," Winnie scoffed, and Mary gave her a pointed look.

"The way she walks," Margie added.

"And her clothes aren't elegant or dignified," Winnie added. "And aren't Middle Eastern women supposed to have more decorum?" she asked in a matter-of-fact 'this is not a question' tone.

Mary laughed. "This is the 1950s, ladies. The world is moving on. Didn't you know this is the day of 'Angry Young Men' and Beatniks?"

The girls exchanged condescending glances and Winnie, setting the presence of her leadership over the three girls, said, "We don't move in such circles, Lady Mary." Her expression was so serious Mary had to stifle a smile.

"Of course you don't," Mary said, realizing she'd been too flippant herself, "but a young woman who, no doubt, has traveled around the world with her father may have broader ideas that don't quite align with ours."

"Perhaps you're right, Lady Mary," Margie said with a warm smile. "Maybe *we* are a step behind the times and Jezebel is just showing us the future of princesses."

Dotty twirled in her gown. She danced herself a few feet away with a big toothy grin on her face as she observed the crowd. Mary wasn't entirely sure if the girl was daft, or was she, as Mary hoped, secretly collecting conversational information?

"Now, ladies," Mary said, "I'm going to call the class to order, and I'll remind them all of how things are done in the company of royalty. Then we'll begin seeing how everyone proceeds up the room to meet the Queen, which will be me today, of course."

Mary grinned as Margie giggled.

7

INVITATIONS

Once again, by the end of the afternoon, Mary was resting in the morning room. Each and every one of the ladies were of their own mind on how things should be done, and they weren't shy about expressing it. All of the stubbornness served to remind Mary she was from an older generation and possibly out-of-touch with the modern world—in particular, teenage girls. In truth, Mary was, for the first time, feeling a bit thankful that she'd never had children.

Ponsonby entered the room and delivered his message formally. "Lady Eleanor from the Palace is here, milady."

She noted Ponsonby's coolness toward the secretary and quickly replied, "Show her in, please."

Mary smoothed out the silk overlay of her cotton tube dress, an old favorite of hers. Though a few extra pounds crept into her waistline in recent years, she couldn't help the youthful feeling the soft fabric gave her. She adjusted her position, sitting with legs to the side and ankles crossed, as she awaited her guest.

"Good afternoon, Lady Mary," Eleanor greeted her with an expansive smile made brighter by the twinkle in her eyes. Mary stood as Eleanor leaned forward to kiss cheeks with her and add, "I've come bearing gifts."

"I hope it's a large glass of sherry," Mary replied and sat back down. "I didn't realize how tiring it would be training young people."

Eleanor laughed softly. "It isn't alcohol, but there will be drinks. It's an invitation to a soiree the Queen is holding at the Palace. The event was organized some time ago." She paused, frowning. "It's only now we've realized you hadn't received an invitation."

Ponsonby entered and set down a tray of tea.

"Thank you, Ponsonby." Mary said, smiling, and Eleanor nodded.

Ponsonby slid the doors closed as he left, and Eleanor continued, "I do hope you'll come, Lady Mary."

"Since arriving in town, I've noticed a shopping trip is in order." She smoothed her hand over the silk overlay again. "I'm sadly in need of a new wardrobe." Mary let out a deep breath, the final straw in her determination to *get with the times*, as the young girls in her charge might say.

Eleanor sipped her tea.

Mary made her decision. "Your timing is perfect. I'd be happy to join the soiree. When is it?"

"Tonight, I'm afraid." Eleanor flashed Mary a sympathetic smile. "As I said, my mistake was not spotting this when you agreed to take up the post. However, there's a fine new shop in the Royal Arcade. I'll forward you their address and telephone number." She handed Mary an embossed invitation card.

Mary surveyed the details. "Tonight. Yes, I'm certainly free once the matter of the new finery is resolved."

"I'll send a car for you, of course," Eleanor said.

"Thank you," Mary hesitated before adding, "Also, would

you recommend a shop to mend my handbag?" She grimaced at the thought of the man in the park trying to murder her.

"I'll telephone you an address the moment I'm back in my office. There is a new shop on Pearl Street that specializes in matching your wardrobe with the perfect accessories—gloves, shoes, and handbags. Shall I just make the appointments for you?"

"Yes. That will be kind. Give the details of the appointment to Ponsonby, and he will see that I arrive on time. My pupils depart at three p.m. each afternoon." Mary sipped her tea calmly enough, but inside, she felt life anew, and all because she was excited to be refreshing her wardrobe.

"There are more events," Eleanor said. "I've brought invitations for the next two weeks." She set down her tea and retrieved a small stack of cards that she handed to Mary. "Let me know which you can attend, and I'll arrange cars and anything else you might need."

"I'll be at all of them if I can," Mary said, smiling.

"Mother will be at some too. You'll be able to catch up," Eleanor replied before nibbling one of Cook's excellent Shrewsbury biscuits.

Mary observed Eleanor's graceful movements and hoped all her students would look like that by the end of her tutelage in May.

LATER THAT EVENING, Lady Mary looked around this grand salon of Buckingham Palace in satisfaction. Everything was as it should be, save for her new dress, an amber metallic print dress layered under a thick faux fur shawl that the shop owner insisted was the "height of fashion." Even though Mary knew enough about current trends, she wasn't entirely convinced of its beauty, particularly the faux fur. It may be the *new* thing, but real fur was infinitely better.

This evening, she had a pep in her step. Her new wardrobe provided a dignified look for a mature woman. There was no way she was trying to squeeze her nearly sixty-year-old body into a cocktail dress. Not even for a royal occasion.

Elegance and refinement trimmed every detail of the evening. Taking her back to the good old days again, a familiar warmth of nostalgia resonated within. *The royals really know how to put on an event.*

Eleanor approached, smiling and signaling a servant to hand Mary a drink. "I'm so pleased you're here, Your Grace. I must help you find some old friends." She paused. "And even some new ones."

"Thank you. I was just admiring the room and the guests. Everything looks as it did in my day." Mary had been about to say in the good old days and realized that wouldn't be polite. To Eleanor and most of the people in the room, these *were* the good days.

Eleanor sipped her drink. "The public rooms have all been restored. In the background, there's still a lot of the Palace that needs additional updating. You should visit my office in winter."

"I don't see many of my old friends," Mary said, looking around. "Are we all retired from public life?"

"Tonight's gathering is for people working on current events," Eleanor replied. "You'll reunite with your old circle at some of the others, but let me introduce you to the event staff for the debs ball. You'll need to go over the details to be sure the girls know what to expect."

As they weaved their way through small knots of people chatting in hushed tones, Mary thought mischievously, *I've not had enough to drink yet.*

"The only differences are the room and the girls, really," Eleanor continued, "but it's best if you meet and talk."

As the evening grew later, Mary was decidedly ready to leave. Everyone was very polite, but she couldn't help thinking the age difference weighed heavily on the minds of those she talked to. She was almost certainly the oldest person in the room, though the errant thought passed through her mind that her predecessor, Lady Hilary, would likely have felt the same.

"Lady Mary."

A voice caught her attention, and Mary turned to glimpse a middle-aged woman approaching her.

"Yes?" Mary said, searching her mind for a name to fit the face.

"You don't know me," the woman said, kindness exuding from her smile. "I'm Ambassador Bamford's wife, Patricia."

Mary shook the outstretched hand, smiling politely in return.

"I've only just learned you're tutoring the debutantes for the ball this year," Patricia said.

"Oh," Mary said. "Is one of my students a relation of yours?"

"No, nothing like that," Patricia replied, "but I do know Princess Jezebel from the time my husband was ambassador in Tzatzikistan. We often met Jezebel at King Raheem's court. I'd dearly like to meet her again. It's been over ten years now. I was very fond of her when she was little, such a beautiful child and so friendly."

Would Jezebel be as eager to reunite with Mrs. Bamford? The only conclusion Mary came to was that she didn't know the princess well enough to make an informed decision.

"I'll have to ask Princess Jezebel," she said at last. "There may be protocols imposed on her time by her father. Let me have your card in case arrangements can be made."

"I understand," Patricia said, opening her evening purse and producing a white and gold visiting card.

"Either myself or Ponsonby, my butler, will telephone you tomorrow," Mary promised, putting the card in her new purse, a subdued basket weave with tiny beads at each weaved intersection.

Though tiring, the evening had been a great boost to Mary's spirit, especially coming after the near-murder in the park. Back in the comfort of her room, she fell fast asleep dreaming of adventure, car racing, and flights of fancy with her dearly departed husband, Roland.

As the young women arrived that afternoon, Mary walked the room greeting each one individually, hoping to catch Jezebel before she became entwined in conversation. After overhearing youthful conversations about fashion faux pas, she saw Jezebel stepping out of the embassy car and making her way up the steps.

"Good afternoon, Jezebel," Mary greeted. "May I have a moment of your time before you join the others?"

Mary guided the Princess into the small room off the entrance hall where they could be alone. Ponsonby dutifully closed the door behind them.

"What is it?" Jezebel asked, acting nonchalantly though a concerned look crossed her face.

As always, Mary was puzzled by the woman's lack of grace.

"It's nothing, my dear," Mary said, thinking the princess was concerned that she'd done something wrong. "In fact, I hope it will be something good for you." She paused to await a response from Jezebel. After a moment of awkward silence, Mary continued, "I met Mrs. Bamford at a function last evening. Her husband was the British ambassador to your father's court some years ago, and she says she knew you as a child."

Again, Mary paused, but this time there was a delayed response.

"I hardly remember her," Jezebel said slowly. "I must've been very young."

"Seven or eight, I imagine," Mary said. "She said it was ten years ago."

Jezebel shrugged, which irritated Mary. *Ladies do not shrug. Has she learned nothing of the three Ds?*

"Well, I was afraid that might be the case," Mary said. "Mrs. Bamford asked if she could join us for tea one afternoon. She has fond memories of you and would like to visit with you."

Jezebel frowned. "Do I have to?"

"Not if you don't want to," Mary said, "but it would be for the best if you did. I'm sure your father would want you to make every effort to make friends here in London."

Jezebel's expression remained sullen. "Yes, I'm sure he would. Then tell her to come... but not this afternoon. I must leave immediately after the lessons today."

Mary smiled. "I will telephone her this evening and arrange something for tomorrow or the next day. That way, it will be over quickly, and you can focus on preparing for the ball."

"The day after tomorrow would be best," Jezebel said, still frowning, "I'm also busy tomorrow evening."

"I'll relay the message to Mrs. Bamford."

Mary ushered Jezebel to return to the ballroom. Mary shook her head over the likely success of the proposed tea, hoping Jezebel would remember Mrs. Bamford when the time came and that all would go well.

8

IN THE NEWS

The following evening, after another demanding day's practice which Jezebel again hurried away from, Mary strolled the gardens with Barkley at her heel before returning to the drawing room for tea.

"I do love this Darjeeling blend, Ponsonby." Mary looked up from her teacup. Recognizing familiar signs of a disturbance by Ponsonby's grim facial expression and extra stiff stance, Mary asked, "What is it?"

"I'll pass on your approval to Cook, milady," Ponsonby said. "There's bad news. The woman you told me about yesterday, Mrs. Patricia Bamford, was murdered last night. It was on the radio news this morning."

"What?" Mary cried. "Are you sure it's the same woman?"

"Tonight's evening papers will give more details, I'm sure," Ponsonby replied, "but the radio said she was the wife of Sir Humphrey Bamford, who had recently retired from the diplomatic service. It must be the same woman."

"Bring me all tonight's newspapers," Mary said. "Every one of them."

"I'll go out and buy the ones we don't normally receive, milady."

"This is incredible," Mary murmured. "What motive could anyone have?" she asked, not realizing Ponsonby was still awaiting his signal to depart.

"The radio spoke of robbery," Ponsonby replied. "Most unlikely. I'm sure the lady wouldn't go anywhere that robbers might be met with."

"Yesterday I might have agreed if not for that awful business in the park. You don't think..." Mary trailed off.

"It's unlikely that this would be the same man who attacked you," Ponsonby added before exiting on Mary's cue.

She picked up her needlework, working in her mind the peculiar goings-on over the last few days while she stitched a delicate embroidered flower into a handkerchief. She was a day behind on this sampler for tomorrow's embroidery lesson. The ball didn't strictly need anyone to be good at embroidery, but Lady Hilary had included it in the plan. She stitched until Ponsonby brought in the evening newspapers on a large silver tray.

Setting the tray down on the table, Ponsonby paused waiting for her to speak.

Mary asked, "Have you read them all?"

"Yes, milady. All of the papers confirmed Patricia Bamford. Some suggest she'd strayed into an unsafe part of the city."

Mary perused the top paper, reading the murderous headline. "Get Chief Superintendent Griffiths on the telephone for me, please. We need to know more."

Thirty minutes and five small, woven, embroidery roses later, Ponsonby connected Mary with DCS Griffiths.

"Good evening, Lady Mary. I have only a minute. I've just come from a crime scene, and I'm expected elsewhere immediately."

In Mary's mind, she could envision the weariness creasing his forehead, just from the tone of his voice. "I appreciate it's late in the evening for you, Chief Superintendent, so I'll be brief. I assure you this isn't an idle call."

"I hope not," Griffiths replied.

"You see, just yesterday, Patricia Bamford and I had organized an afternoon tea for tomorrow."

"So you may have been one of the last people to speak with her," Griffiths stated. "I'd like to talk to you about this in the morning."

"I was going to suggest that," Mary said. "Shall I expect you early?"

"I'll arrive around seven-thirty."

"I'll alert the staff. Thank you, Chief Superintendent."

Not sure what implications her meeting with Patricia Bamford might have had, Mary replayed the conversation in her mind. Nothing that had been said in their conversation helped her understand what was happening.

Frustrated, she abandoned her needlework and prepared for bed early. As she did, she considered what she would say to Jezebel the next day. This murder was disquieting, not just because of the woman's death but because she'd been killed so soon after making an appointment to tea with the princess. Mary shivered as she pondered that before turning out her bedside lamp.

THE NEXT MORNING, after a sleepless night, Mary put on her best face before descending to the breakfast room.

Two sips into her glass of orange juice, Ponsonby announced, "Detective Chief Superintendent Griffiths, milady."

He made the introduction with all the formality usually reserved for royalty.

Mary stifled a smile knowing Ponsonby and Griffiths were wary of each other. Ponsonby's stiffness only furthered the tension.

"Good morning," Mary said, taking Griffiths' outstretched hand. "This is a sad business."

"True," Griffiths said, letting go of Mary's hand and taking the proffered chair, "but you being involved in the case is an added bonus... unless you did it, of course." He smiled, and the slightest dimple formed in his long, angular cheek.

Mary gestured to Ponsonby, who was still standing, to take a seat, knowing how much it would irritate his fine sense of what was due to a duchess. Stony-faced, he sat facing Mary and Griffiths.

"I know your tendency to tease us poor amateurs, Chief Superintendent, so I won't dignify your sally with a response," Mary said, smiling. "I was pleased to take on this post but not so desperate to put my predecessor out of the way."

"I had no doubts on that score," Griffiths said.

Mary's thoughts strayed back to former days, but they were no longer young, and now he was the officer in charge, one who was willing to listen when so many wouldn't.

"Now, Chief Superintendent, what would you like to know?"

"Everything that you know, Lady Mary," Griffiths said, "but perhaps we can start with the reason for your meeting with the victim."

Mary explained the background and the events leading up to her arranging the afternoon tea between the princess and Mrs. Bamford.

Griffiths' normally impassive features grew grave as she spoke. When she finished, he said, "Diplomats, royalty, and international relations... a trilogy of contrivances that gum up the best investigations."

"We've no reason to suspect any foreign involvement, have we?" Mary replied. "We read in the local papers it was a robbery gone wrong."

Griffiths shook his head. "Her jewelry and rings, valuables that a thief would abscond with, were untouched. They did steal money but left more costly items."

"Are you claiming that the press has misled us as they so often do when they can get away with it?" Mary had herself experienced many hurtful articles over the years and had a low opinion of the press.

"Wrong assumptions wouldn't be a first," Griffiths agreed.

"I'm sure you've thought of this, but maybe they decided the personal items would be too hard to sell," Mary suggested.

"Yes, we've given consideration to that, but I'm not convinced," Griffiths replied. "To be honest, I don't believe the stolen money was anything other than a poor attempt to make a murder *look* like a robbery, which is why I'm both pleased to learn what you've told me and also dismayed to find so many difficult alternatives."

"Can you tell us more about the murder? As you know, we," Mary said, gesturing to Ponsonby, "have doubts about the death of my predecessor. This new murder must be connected somehow."

"There isn't much to say," Griffiths replied. "The victim was walking her dog in the park, which she did every evening at that time when she was stabbed in the back. Her body was left in the grass where it fell and discovered by another dog walker some-time later."

"Is it possibly the same man who attacked me only two nights ago?" Mary asked.

"I entertained the possibility there was a link," Griffiths said.

"However, with so little to go on in both instances, it's hard to come to any firm conclusion. This man attacked from behind. Your attacker did not. The weapon in this case was a large knife with a curved blade, a very serious weapon, whereas the man who attacked you used an ordinary steak knife found in any good restaurant."

"I see."

"If I may," Ponsonby interjected, "the attacker could be someone who wasn't in the habit of attacking people with knives and simply learned his lesson after his failure with Lady Mary. This knife may be one he stole rather than taking another from the restaurant where he works or eats."

Griffiths nodded. "We thought of that too. Still, you do see why we can't assume it's the same man, even though we rarely have any knife-related crimes in London and, even more rarely, attacks on women of the upper circles in society."

"It is a mystery," Mary said. "However, I'm convinced these two incidents, the knife attacks, I mean, are linked. It can hardly be otherwise, even if there are two different would-be murderers..." Mary paused. "And weapons."

"The question *that* raises is even more unlikely, though," Griffiths said. "Why? Why would someone be murdering women linked to the debutante ball? Why now, when it's been going on for centuries without incident?"

"I feel the princess is at the root of it," Ponsonby said. "I don't mean she's personally involved, but something about her presence is a problem to someone."

Griffiths nodded thoughtfully, but Mary said, "With that speculation, then my predecessor's death couldn't be part of it. She died before the princess's visit was generally known."

"Maybe her death wasn't part of it," Griffiths said. "Maybe she really did just die accidentally."

"Of a poison that somehow got onto her scarf?" Ponsonby made a very undignified scoffing noise.

Mary shook her head. "It's too coincidental. They must be linked. We just need to find the link."

The three lapsed into thoughtful silence as each considered the possibilities until Cook entered the room with a breakfast trolley and began placing dishes on the sideboard.

Mary asked, "Chief Superintendent, may we view the files on my predecessor's death? There may be clues that *we* can pick up, viewing the information from a different perspective that you and your colleagues aren't aware of."

Griffiths nodded. "And in exchange, I'll need you to give me an account of the details of what's been happening here: your attack, the ball, the princess's behavior, and the ambassador's wife's death." He waved his hand slightly. "It's also possible *we* might have a different perspective that you aren't aware of."

"Very clever, Inspector."

She respected Griffiths. He was a keen investigator, above all others she'd met in those early years.

"Ponsonby and I will write our statements this morning," Mary said. "If you drop by this afternoon with copies of your files, we can make the exchange."

"I'll do that," he said, rising from his chair.

"You must eat, Chief Superintendent," Mary urged.

He smiled. "I've already had my breakfast, thank you. I should go. I've a lot of work to do this morning." He was almost at the door when he turned and said, "I almost forgot. Your gardener will have some help for the next few weeks."

"You're placing one of your men on my staff?" Mary asked, torn between amusement and annoyance. She really didn't know whether to be offended at his high-handedness or grateful for it.

He shook his head, grinning. "Not me," he said, grinning.

"MI5 have decided to get closer to the event preparations. They get nervous when the Sovereign is in a vulnerable situation."

"So, in fact, my gardener will get no help at all," Mary said, smiling.

"Actually, he might. Apparently, the young man *is* a gardener, or at least he has experience and knowledge. His father is one of these country gentlemen who is always trying to improve the breed and yield of everything, so I'm told."

"That will be a treat for old Mr. Jobson," Mary said dryly. "He was against any improvements when Roland was alive. The two of them had many long discussions about how the gardens should be managed, and I don't believe Roland won a single one of them."

9

DOGS AND BUTLERS

Later that morning, when Mary and Ponsonby had compared their statements, which they'd written separately to ensure nothing was copied or missed, Mary said, "When we were talking earlier, I suggested the princess couldn't be the catalyst because my predecessor's death happened before anyone knew the princess was coming to the ball. Now, I'm unsure."

"The way I see it, milady, someone may have known the princess was to attend," Ponsonby suggested. "Someone connected to the embassy, perhaps."

Mary nodded. "That's true, and I was thinking about it as I wrote my statement. We should observe the princess a little more closely."

"And our three amateur sleuths?" Ponsonby asked. "Are they still puzzled about the princess?"

"They are," Mary replied. "Has Barkley met the Princess?"

"He has. Barkley doesn't like her either, and I trust all four of their instincts," Ponsonby said. His tone hardened as he continued, "On a number of occasions, he's accompanied me to the door when she and the others arrived. Barkley reacts differently to her, even more aggressively, perhaps, than he does to the others he doesn't like."

"It may be that the princess hasn't lived around dogs all her life, the way we do here in England," Mary said. "Dogs can sense when they're not liked."

"That's possible, of course," Ponsonby said, "and I'm not saying Barkley is our final arbiter, but he did sense your attacker's presence long before you did."

"They say dogs can tell who is a good person and who isn't," Mary said, smiling fondly at her furry companion who was lazing by the fire.

"Quite so," Ponsonby said. "And don't forget our young colleagues' views."

Mary shook her head. "I don't, though I do think they're just expecting a stereotypical young woman from the Middle East and are suspicious to find her to be as modern as they are. What's your view, Ponsonby?"

"I agree with the young women," he replied. "She's like someone acting the role of a princess."

"But she must be the princess," Mary said. "She is staying at her country's embassy. People like the princess are checked out by the Special Branch and the secret service. There's no way she isn't who she says she is."

"I agree, but she still doesn't feel right, if I may put it that way."

"How does one know that someone isn't quite right? I'm sure I don't."

"With respect, milady, you're not a butler."

Mary laughed. "Fortunately for me, I'm not. I'd have starved to death waiting for my first position."

"Then you're happy for the three young sleuths, Barkley, and I to investigate the princess more closely?"

"Of course, but make sure none of you offend her," Mary

said. "Our government will be quite angry if we cause a diplomatic incident."

"Before involving the young ladies, you should warn them not to upset the princess," Ponsonby said.

"I'll do that when they arrive," Mary agreed. "Now, we need to prepare for their arrival while we wait for DCS Griffiths to return with his files."

WHEN GRIFFITHS ARRIVED, the exchange of files and statements was expeditious. Each of the three—Mary, Ponsonby, and Griffiths—scanned the documents to look for items where they might need additional explanation.

"This is clear enough, Chief Superintendent," Mary said when Ponsonby looked up from the file and nodded his acceptance. "Now, how can we help each other to solve this case?"

"I'm not sure we can, Your Grace," Griffiths said. "I can't give my full time to this new death. However, your statement may be invaluable to my team in determining if it is a murder related to the ball. I hope the papers I've just given will help you, but beyond liaising with each other regularly, there won't be much else I will be doing here."

Mary frowned. "Ponsonby and I, however, can't leave the investigation hanging. If nothing else, my own life may be in danger if our suspicions are correct."

"You wouldn't accept my offer of a man to guard you personally," Griffiths said, "but I've spoken to the local police station and warned them there may be trouble ahead."

Mary nodded. "We might need police assistance, if there's any physical violence, I mean."

"We must hope it doesn't come to that," Griffiths teased her, "and you should act in a way to make sure it doesn't happen, like leaving all this to the police."

"You were happy to have my help years ago, I recall," Mary said sharply.

"You may remember your last *case*," Griffiths said seriously, pausing for emphasis, "where you and your sister sleuths were almost entirely wrong, but if you find anything this time, I'll be happy to learn of it. After all, you were right on multiple occasions."

Only a little mollified, Mary said, "You should also tell the people who guard the foreign dignitaries that Princess Jezebel may be in danger or may be mixed up in something criminal." Her tone revealed her diminishing composure.

Griffiths nodded. "I can tell them the princess may be in danger. However, they know their job better than I do. If I'm too pushy, they'll soon tell me where to go."

Ponsonby let Griffiths out.

When he was gone, Mary questioned, "Ponsonby, can we obtain a recent photo of the princess? Not a photo of the woman we meet every day, but one taken at her school in Switzerland or one taken in her own country?"

"I'll do my best," Ponsonby said. "It would indeed be a good starting place for our own investigation."

As Ponsonby left, Mary gazed out the window, turning her suspicions over in her mind. Their ideas had led to the wild speculation that Jezebel could be an imposter, but what if she wasn't an imposter and was just a daughter or a daughter gone rogue? Young people were throwing off the inhibitions of the past and demanding a different future all over the Western world today. Had Jezebel fallen into that fatal way of life and thinking? Was Jezebel herself the source of their unease? Only time, and additional investigations, would confirm or denounce their suspicions.

THE NEXT DAY, Mary gathered her three assistant sleuths at Culpeper House before the afternoon class and explained what she wanted from them and how they must behave.

"We understand, Lady Mary," Winnie said impatiently. "We're not completely hopeless, but it isn't just the princess."

"What do you mean?" Mary asked.

"Some of the others aren't quite right as well," Margie said, "and Barkley agrees. You should see how he bristles at that red-headed girl."

Mary frowned. "Now, ladies, I hope this isn't just old-fashioned snobbery. Not everyone to be presented comes from the top drawer, it's true. Their fathers are in professions or even trade, but that isn't an excuse to act unkindly toward them."

The three ladies protested immediately, with Winnie saying, "We're just saying that to single out Jezebel for investigation when there are others who are also suspicious doesn't seem right."

"You can't investigate everyone," Mary protested.

"May I make a suggestion?" Ponsonby asked.

"Yes. What is it?" Mary asked.

"I propose we use Barkley's instinct as a starting point. That is, the people Barkley is suspicious of are the ones we start with."

Mary looked at the three, who were nodding in agreement.

"Dogs know things about people," Margie said, looking down at the snoozing pooch. "I agree with this plan."

Mary relaxed her stance. "Very well. We'll start there."

Talking excitedly, the three young ladies left the room on their way to meet the arriving debutantes with Barkley, now fully awake, in tow.

"I do hope they will be careful," Mary said to Ponsonby. "I'd like to repeat my role as 'debutante trainer' again next year."

Ponsonby smiled. "The role has certainly taken a great financial weight off your shoulders."

Mary nodded. "The salary alone is worth it, but more than that, it's given me a renewed sense of purpose. I hadn't realized how low in spirit I'd become."

"I'll observe the greetings," Ponsonby said, moving toward the door.

"No," Mary said. "Let me do that today. I want to watch Barkley's attitude toward each of them."

"I'll make myself scarce by assisting Cook select today's vegetables from the garden."

"Cook will love that," Mary said, smiling mischievously. "Having you to help with the vegetables, I mean."

Moments after he'd left, she heard the faintest grumble from Cook as Ponsonby disappeared into the lower regions.

Mary and Barkley positioned themselves near the door when the students began arriving. She watched as Barkley ran to greet some and was stroked and patted in return. He growled softly at some, who didn't give him a wink of attention. Ponsonby was right. Barkley did prefer some and dislike others. Mary had never seen him quite so sure in his likes and dislikes as he was with the debutantes. When Jezebel arrived, however, Barkley's growling rose dramatically.

"Quiet, Barkley," Mary said before Jezebel had walked far enough into the room to overhear Barkley's opinion.

Jezebel, however, eyed Barkley with equal animosity.

"Jezebel." Mary spoke quietly. "We must talk." She ushered the princess into a nearby room and started to close the door.

"Don't let that dog come in," Jezebel said sharply. "He doesn't like me."

"Oh, Barkley's harmless."

"We do not approve of dogs in my country," Jezebel replied.

"I see. Then we will send him away."

Seeing Ponsonby had returned and was hovering in the hall, she motioned him over to take Barkley. When he obliged, Mary closed the door.

"Have you heard the news, Princess?"

Jezebel looked puzzled, and her brow furrowed. "I don't take notice of such things."

"I'm sorry to be the bearer of this terrible news, but I must inform you that the lady who remembered you as a child and who was coming to visit for tea was murdered last night."

Jezebel transitioned through several facial expressions before landing on what Mary viewed as uncertainty. "I'm sorry to hear that," she said at last. "I don't remember her, yet I am sad."

"Death is always horrible," Mary said solemnly. "In this case, it seems senseless. Do you feel able to continue with today's practice?"

"Of course," Jezebel said. "I'm a princess. I must be brave." She spoke firmly, but Mary noticed the girl's hands trembling, and the color had drained from her face.

Mary nodded approvingly. "Quite right. That's the spirit. Well, let us join the others before they begin to act as though they have a holiday today."

AT THE END of the day's lessons, Mary waited for the last of the debutantes to leave then turned to Ponsonby and her three assistants and said, "You're right. Barkley does not like the princess."

There was a chorus of agreement from the girls.

"But he doesn't like a number of the others either," Mary continued. "We need to be sure we look into all their backgrounds and not become fixated on just one of them."

"But we know the others," Margie said. "They may not all be real ladies, but they aren't suspicious characters."

"It's true," Winnie said, "and many are just frightened of dogs, like my friend Penny."

Mary laughed as they made their way to the afternoon sitting room where they always had tea after the classes ended. "Your reasons for excluding your friends and the others may be valid, but we can't allow ourselves to lose sight of the fact it isn't only Jezebel who Barkley doesn't like, and we agreed to use his response to them as our starting point."

Ponsonby coughed discreetly and waited for Mary's attention. When she nodded, he said, "If I may say so, Lady Mary, I've thought more about this and now feel we're putting too much faith in Barkley's instincts."

"It was your idea to begin with, Ponsonby," Mary stated.

"Our sleuthing team, however, has made a good point," Ponsonby said. "They have known many, if not all, the others since they were children. The princess is not known to any of us."

The girls bobbed their heads in agreement, and Winnie spoke up. "Lady Mary, there's not more than five of the others we haven't known since our first boarding schools."

Mary frowned. "But Jezebel is staying at the embassy with the ambassador. How could he or his wife or the staff not know who she is? And how could she be an imposter when she traveled from her home to here with an official escort? I can't agree that she is in any way different from your friends."

Ponsonby gave his inevitable discreet cough again, this time without waiting for permission to interject. "We don't even know ·vhat the situation really is. We know two women have been killed and you, Lady Mary, were attacked, but we don't know why. It still may have nothing to do with the debutantes or the ball at all."

"It must have," the trio of junior sleuths said in unison.

"If it doesn't," Lady Mary said as they helped themselves to the snacks and tea awaiting them in the morning room, "we have to believe someone is targeting rich women who move in very select circles and who have some connection to the ball, even a connection as small as just asking to meet one of the debutantes."

Ponsonby voiced his reason, "The position you hold, Lady Mary, was held earlier by Lady Hilary and isn't well-known. It isn't published anywhere, and no one could have known Mrs. Bamford wanted to meet the princess, except you, the princess, and Mrs. Bamford herself, unless she told others."

"I do see what you're driving at, Ponsonby," Mary said thoughtfully. "I hardly told anyone about the meeting, though Mrs. Bamford may have." She shook her head. "I just can't grasp how any explanation other than Queen Charlotte's Ball makes sense."

"Why would anyone kill over the ball?" Margie asked. "Lots of people don't like it anymore, but that doesn't mean it's worth killing over."

"I agree with Lady Mary," Winnie said. "It has to be the ball. Nothing else connects the deaths and the attack."

"Nothing that we know of," Ponsonby said. "We made this connection because we're a part of it. There may be other connections we don't understand yet. After all, the three ladies who were attacked are all in the same circle of society. They're not random."

"Unless they are," Dotty replied for the first time in the conversation.

All eyes darted in her direction.

"There's no such thing as a coincidence," Winne interjected confidently, to which Dotty nodded in her unconcerned way.

"All of which," Mary said firmly, "leads me to repeat what I said. I want us to investigate everyone—the debutantes and the victims. We'll find out if anything new turns up."

"We have to make a plan," Margie suggested.

"I thought of that," Dotty spoke up again. "I know ten of the others really well. We went to the same school. I can question them and look further into their backgrounds, but I already know that none of them are anything but what they appear."

"You can't start with that in your mind," Winnie cried, "or you'll miss things, like where do they go for their holidays or other places you don't encounter them. You have to have an open mind."

"*We* should *not* investigate the ones we've known all our lives," Margie said, frowning. "As Winnie said, we'll miss things a stranger would see."

"I won't miss anything," Dotty said crossly. "If we have to start from scratch, we won't be finished by Christmas." A petulant frown grew on her face.

"Dotty has a point," Winnie said, nodding. "How can we do this quickly without skipping over gaps?"

"If I may, ladies," Ponsonby said, "I suggest you meet daily and review what you've gathered about each individual and each of you questions the other two, cross-referencing your information."

"I like that," Dotty replied.

"And I can investigate Lady Hilary's life further," Winnie suggested. "She and my mother were very close."

"Who could look into Mrs. Bamford's background?" Margie asked. When no one answered immediately, she continued, "Then I'll try. I have an uncle who was in the diplomatic service. He may know the Bamfords."

"'*Who's Who* is always a good place to start," Dotty replied, her attention waning and her gaze pointed off in the distance. "*The Times* would have information too."

"Then let's get to it," Mary said, dismissing them.

As they trailed out, Mary sat back with her arms folded in her lap, pleased her new sleuths were taking the initiative with very little direction from her.

THAT EVENING, Mary was preparing for another event at the Palace, described by the invitation as a "small evening affair," when she heard the telephone ring.

I hope this isn't a cancellation.

All of the mystery and intrigue had her feeling quite spry.

When she heard Ponsonby making his way upstairs, Mary slipped a robe over herself before calling, "Who is it, Ponsonby?"

He stopped outside her bedroom door and said, "Detective Chief Superintendent Griffiths, milady. He wants to tell you of some changes being made to the princess's routine."

Further intrigued, Mary hurried downstairs and picked up the handset. Short of breath, she said, "Yes, Chief Superintendent?"

"Good evening, Your Grace," Griffiths said. "The secret service took your information more seriously than I thought they would. They intend to discreetly restrict access to the princess until they have made themselves comfortable that she's in no danger."

"Oh, bother," Mary said. "She won't like that. I hope she doesn't take offense and upset the diplomatic apple cart."

"I'm sure they've managed these situations many times before," Griffiths said. "My calling here was to warn you that any strange men loitering outside your house while the princess is in attendance are likely to be either Special Branch or MI5 men and not dangerous revolutionaries."

"I understand. Thank you."

"How did the princess take the news of Mrs. Bamford's death?" Griffiths asked.

"Calmly," Mary replied, "but..."

"But?"

"I think she was very shocked or possibly very frightened." She described Jezebel's trembling hands and ashen face.

"You think that means she told people and this was the result?" he asked.

"That's one possibility," Mary said. "The other is she has just realized her own danger for the first time. She *is* very young, after all."

"Murder is a frightening event, it's true," Griffiths said, "particularly when we first come close to it. It probably means nothing, as you say."

He rang off, and Mary returned to her room, deep in contemplation. Ponsonby was hovering at the head of the stairs as she arrived.

"Did he tell you?" Mary asked.

Ponsonby nodded. "About the increased security, yes, milady. I fear we're in for fireworks in the coming days when the princess realizes what's happening."

10

A NEW GARDENER

Remembering her shortness of breath the previous evening, Mary picked at her breakfast like a bird. An anxious Cook had provided a hearty meal. Mary stood to leave the table when she found Ponsonby waiting to speak to her.

"I was miles away," Mary said, smiling. "What is it?"

"I've made a list of the girls Barkley doesn't like and cross-checked it with the list of names our young sleuths identified when we spoke yesterday," Ponsonby said, handing her a single sheet of paper. "The two lists are close, as you can see."

Mary scanned the list and quickly nodded at the similarities. Of the fifty debutantes, Barkley was suspicious of ten, and the girls had named eight. Only one from the girls' list wasn't on Barkley's list.

"We concentrate on the ten, then," Mary said. "The one our sleuths don't like but Barkley is happy with is the girl who wears too much scent."

"Yes, milady. Most unfortunate," he said, wrinkling his nose. "Her presence makes Barkley sneeze, but he doesn't growl at her the way he does others."

"So Barkley doesn't distinguish her as a problem," Mary said.

"He sees past the facade to the character beneath. You linked the investigating assistant to the names, I see."

"Yes, milady," Ponsonby said. "As you see, two of our assistant sleuths have three to investigate, and one, Winnie, has four."

Mary considered for a moment. "That will work out well. Winnie is the most forward of them. We must investigate all of the names quickly. Time is running out. Less than two weeks to go and if Queen Charlotte's Ball is in any danger, we need to know sooner rather than later."

"While it may be incredible," Ponsonby said, "I think, to move quickly, we must assume that the motive *is* the ball and not some other unknown."

"Well, lunatics do exist." Mary chuckled. "We can't entirely rule it out, just as we can't rule out that it really does have something to do with Jezebel and, as a result, will only happen at the ball."

"I'm expecting photographs of the princess today, milady," Ponsonby reminded her.

"You've found some?"

"Detective Chief Superintendent Griffiths has," Ponsonby said, "and one of my fellow butlers is engaged in a family that spent time out there. He has been given permission to have the photographs copied, and they will arrive later today."

"It would be useful if they arrived before the girls all left for the day," Mary suggested.

"The images from the police might," Ponsonby said. "I will bring them to you immediately. Having the photos and the princess together may be enough to allay any suspicion."

"But you think not?" Mary questioned.

"If she's an imposter," Ponsonby began, "and I know that's impossible, but if she is, she'll have been chosen because of her strong resemblance. I fear old photos won't be enough to finally answer the question."

Mary nodded. "I know. Only we must do something, and it's as good a place as any to start."

"Quite so," Ponsonby agreed. "Will you keep the list, or should I put it somewhere safe?"

"I'll keep it," Mary replied. "I want it with me when I see the girls today. It will focus my mind."

When Ponsonby left the room, Mary studied the list again.

"Is it ten red herrings or nine red herrings and a pike?" she whispered to herself.

Her soft words made Barkley's keen ears prick up. When nothing interesting happened, he lay down again in front of the fire where he'd been keeping guard since Cook, acting as chambermaid, had lit it earlier.

The police photographs of the princess in her younger days arrived first, as Ponsonby had suspected they would. Mary had them in hand as Jezebel arrived. Discreetly, Mary glanced between the photos and Jezebel as the princess talked with the other debutantes. As they'd feared, the photos—from newspaper clippings—weren't sufficient to confirm her identity.

Family photos, arriving shortly after, provided minimal additional details. While they were clearer, the princess was much younger, not yet even in her teens.

When the debutantes departed for the day, Mary, Ponsonby, Barkley and the three assistant sleuths assembled in the morning room to review their progress. Mary shared the photos.

"The photos don't help," Winnie said, holding one up close to her face before passing them around.

Dotty looked at the photographs. Her face was fixed with a puzzled frown until she finally said, "Her ankles are wrong."

"Her ankles!" Winnie cried out.

Dotty nodded, solid in her opinion. "Look at this photo." She turned a newspaper clipping of "the Princess Jezebel" at a Paris gala, wearing a knee-length skirt. "Her ankles are heavier than the Jezebel we know, aren't they?"

The others studied the photo for a moment, each with their own disbelieving yet curious look on their face.

"They do look thicker," Mary agreed. Remembering her own struggle over breakfast, she said, "Young people often have some 'puppy-fat,' as it's called. Maybe she's lost weight."

Dotty shook her head determinedly. "Not from their ankles, they don't."

"It's only a photo, though," Margie said. "They're never very flattering when you want them to be."

"I agree," Winnie said in a firm tone. "The light, the way she's standing, the clothes and shoes she's wearing, even how long she'd been standing in those heels before the photo was taken could make her ankles look heavier."

Mary frowned. Everything Winnie said was true, of course, and her own instinct was against it, but Dotty had spotted it nonetheless. It was a tiny detail that didn't amount to much, but it still left Jezebel in question.

Poor girl, to be so suspected in a place you'd come to be introduced and should expect to be received with trust and even honor.

Mary sat up in her wingback chair. "Ponsonby?"

His grave expression displayed what she assumed was an aversion to commenting unflatteringly on any young lady's ankles, "I fear none of us look quite like our photos, yet I have to agree with Lady Dorothy." He nodded in her direction. "There does appear to be a slight difference. Whether it's real or not, we haven't enough information to say either way."

"We can take note of it and carry on," Mary replied. "Now, ladies, do any of you have anything to report from your investigations to date?"

Each assistant sleuth provided the details they'd amassed,

information accepted as true. Mary passed the three young girls notebooks to keep track of the clues. Dotty, in her usual distracted manner, inspected the free pen included with the notepad, while the other two girls scrawled their names inside the covers.

The conversation died quickly with very little information and clues.

Mary gave an encouraging smile to each of the girls. "This has been an excellent start, ladies." When she had their full attention, she added, "I do have a small course correction to give you."

The three young ladies came alive with the prospect of a new assignment. *Like Barkley when he hears his name or hears Cook placing his mealtime dish on the floor.*

Mary smiled to herself. "I want you to focus first on this list of names I'm about to give you." She read out the names, and her assistants scrolled them into their notebooks.

"Why these ones first?" Winnie asked.

Mary explained, "We still will do all of them. It's just these names were the ones both you and Barkley identified separately. This will be a good way to be sure we have the most suspicious people investigated first."

"What about Jezebel?" Margie asked. "She's the one we know nothing about."

"We haven't forgotten her. Ponsonby and I are looking into the princess's background. So far, we have nothing concrete to suggest she isn't who she says she is."

"Except her ankles," Dotty replied.

"Yes, except her ankles," Mary agreed begrudgingly.

"Where did you get your new gardener, Lady Mary?" Dotty asked, suddenly changing the subject.

Taken aback, Mary said, "From an agency, I expect. Why?"

Dotty, it seemed, wasn't quite as dreamy-eyed as she looked.

"He's got SA," Margie said, giggling.

Winnie scoffed, "Sex appeal?"

"Even Barkley thinks so," Margie added. "When we arrived, he was watching him work as though besotted."

"Oh, dear," Mary said. "I hope it's that and not Barkley guarding the house against intruders."

The girls laughed.

"No, definitely besotted," Dotty said.

"Well, I don't want you three out there too," Mary said, smiling. "I'm not familiar with our new gardener, but I can't have my students being distracted by young men while we prepare for the ball, nor do I want my gardener distracted when he's supposed to be restoring the garden to its former glory. Cook will be most displeased if she doesn't have a proper herb garden by the weekend."

"Cooks are scary," Margie agreed. "Ours is anyway." She shook her shoulders.

This led to an animated discussion about which of their servants was the grimmest in each house. Mary sent them home still arguing.

LATER THAT EVENING, when Ponsonby brought Mary her drink, she asked, "How are we going to prove Jezebel's authenticity, Ponsonby?"

"We've exhausted the official channels," Ponsonby replied. "They assured us she *is* Princess Jezebel. We need someone who knew her recently, a school friend from that Swiss school or someone from the British Embassy possibly."

"Have none come forward in answer to our *discreet* inquiries?" Mary sipped her sherry.

"No, and we can't do public inquiries," Ponsonby replied. "It would cause too many alerts." Mary looked up to him as he murmured, "It's a great handicap, indeed." A few silent moments later, Ponsonby added, "The school she attended in Switzerland is for royalty, but not British royalty. Do we know any European royals who might assist?"

"I've made inquiries among the few remaining families I know, but the ones I know are all as old as we are," Mary said. "So far, none of them have admitted to having grandchildren at that school."

"Then we must find someone," Ponsonby said. "I'll inquire if any butlers are with families who would know."

"The Butlers' Club is a useful network to have," Mary agreed, warming from her evening drink. A faint flush flashed across her cheeks. "They're in every important household in Europe."

Ponsonby furrowed his brow and said, "Unfortunately, they're also very discreet and hard-pressed to give away the family secrets."

"Just as well," Mary said, thinking of some wild times in her own household that were not much credit to her earlier years.

Mary glanced over at Ponsonby. A glint of something crossed his eyes and a faint smile twitched his lips before he again controlled his facial features.

"However, on this occasion, we aren't asking for family secrets," Ponsonby said, "just who we can talk to about this *finishing school for royals* that Jezebel went to."

"Very clever approach," Mary replied. Her mind was not as sharp as it had been earlier in the day after she had sipped the last of her beverage. She frowned and said, "I find that suspicious in itself. I'd never heard of *The Grimalda School for Young Ladies*. I'm going to have someone visit them in Geneva."

"I fear it will turn out to be quite new, milady," Ponsonby

replied, his tone suggesting this as the worst possible aspect of the establishment. "After all, there wasn't much call for foreign princesses to go to schools in the West until very recently."

"Still, I know someone who just might be able to visit the school. I will contact them in Geneva in the morning."

"Of course, milady." Ponsonby removed her empty glass and awaited her nod before taking his leave.

"Ponsonby," Mary said, "our new gardener, is Barkley besotted with him?"

Ponsonby said, "No more than is appropriate, milady."

"Our assistant sleuths thought he was. I looked out, but the man was nowhere to be seen, and neither was Barkley."

"He does have a way with dogs," Ponsonby agreed. "I believe it's the sign of a nice nature."

"A nice nature is the last thing I need," Mary said, smiling. "He'll have the girls out there too when I need them in here and focused."

"I understand he went to a good school," Ponsonby said.

"It's no matter. See that he doesn't come anywhere near the girls until after the ball." She gave him a knowing look. "I'm relying on you."

Ponsonby nodded.

Mary added, "Just as well. I want to meet this paragon tomorrow."

"Very well, milady."

MARY'S TELEPHONE call to Geneva the next morning brightened her mood. Her friend Sabine was more than willing to do some investigating and gather information on behalf of Mary. With that in motion, Mary was ready to face the day, starting with the new gardener.

She walked casually out into the fresh May morning, calling, "Barkley."

Barkley didn't appear, and she discovered why when she rounded the east wing of the house and saw him digging a hole as the young gardener turned the earth with a spade in one of the old flower beds.

"Hello," Mary said, approaching the two. "You must be our new gardener."

His face lit up in a dazzling smile. "That I am, ma'am."

His words were respectful enough to any chance listener, but Mary could hear the laughter in his voice, and the smile that accompanied it said he was amused by it all.

"Barkley finds your work fascinating," Mary said, nodding down to the digging canine. "I've been calling him for the past five minutes, and I'm sure he heard. I hope you haven't buried a bone for him?"

Barkley looked up when she said "bone." His grin was as engaging as the young man's.

"He and I were chatting," the gardener said. "No bones about, though."

Mary looked around at the flower beds already tidied. "You seem to have persuaded our Mr. Jobson to give you free rein. He's usually very protective of his beds."

"I think he realizes he can't do everything himself at his age," the young worker replied.

There was just enough chill in those words to give Mary a moment of disquiet. "I expect you're right," she said. "How does someone such as yourself come to be a gardener?"

"My father mainly. Sometimes when he was stationed abroad, the family would go along, and we'd bring plants home to experiment with in our gardens. I studied Botany at university, and now that I've graduated, I'm gaining hands-on experience."

"Was your father in the army?" Mary asked.

"Not exactly," he replied guardedly, "but he was often called on by them to assist in matters pertaining to the military. He's a very learned man."

His vague answer left a lot to be followed-up on.

"And you? What do you hope to do?"

"Take over his gardens when he retires. I look forward to a quiet life in the country."

"That sounds admirably peaceful," Mary replied. "We will keep meeting, so I should know your name. I am Lady Mary."

He smiled again. "I know your name. You can call me John."

"Is that your name?"

"One of them," he replied.

"Well, John, it was nice talking to you. Stop that digging, Barkley. We have other work to do."

Barkley looked at John, who smiled and rubbed his head. "We'll talk again later, Barkley. And don't worry about the hole, Lady Mary. I will fill it in."

Barkley turned and followed Mary back to the house. Her thoughts were disturbed by the peculiar hold "John" had over Barkley. Barkley had come to her as a puppy, years ago, from the same kennels where the royal family bought their corgis, and yet here he was, acting as if those years were nothing and "John" was his new master.

It was disturbingly like the way the girls watched "John" as he walked past the ballroom windows. No man should have that kind of power over humans, or canines, Mary thought. *That kind of power can lead people into bad places.*

Once inside, she shook off the eerie feeling she had perceived from the gardener. Her thoughts were convoluted. *He's a gardener, not a future megalomaniac.* Everything about the events of the past weeks was taking her mind into darkness where she shouldn't allow it to go.

She took her coat and hat from the cloakroom and rang the bell for Ponsonby.

"I'm taking Barkley on a walk in the park," she told Ponsonby as he helped her on with her coat. "We both need to get out. Enjoy the bright sunshine."

"Would you like me to accompany you, milady?"

"No," Mary began brusquely then said, "Yes, maybe that would be a good idea." Brooding over her own thoughts wouldn't lighten her mind. "In fact, you should every time until the ball is over."

They headed out and walked toward the park.

Mary asked, "What do we know about our new gardener, Ponsonby?"

"I only know what I told you. He comes from a good family, his father does important work, and he went to a good school."

"He said his father was stationed abroad sometimes," Mary said. "Do we know where?"

"You think maybe Tzatzikistan?"

"It had crossed my mind," Mary replied.

"I will ask through the Butlers' Club," Ponsonby replied. "Maybe you should ask the chief superintendent."

"I will, but he will be told the young man has been thoroughly vetted at the highest level," Mary replied unhappily.

"Only we all know that those traitors Burgess and MacLean were at the *highest* level in our secret service when they fled to Moscow," Ponsonby said.

"Exactly," Mary said. "It's a horrible feeling to think you can't trust anyone."

THE AFTERNOON CLASS was to be deportment, in particular the antique ways the ball insisted the debutantes meet and greet the Queen. Asking twentieth-century young women to behave like nineteenth-century women caused laughter at first then serious grumbling. By the end, Mary became torn between hoping the ball *was* canceled forever and her earlier hope, that she had just shared with Ponsonby, of the ball continuing again next year so she could earn some more money.

"I finally understand what it's like to earn your own income," Mary said, sinking into an easy chair with a full glass of sherry, "and have the hope of security snatched away from you. I'll never again pooh-pooh those news reports that talk about how angry some workers are at their factory closing down."

"Earning your own way in the world *can* give one a sense of great satisfaction," Ponsonby replied.

Mary looked at him quizzically. "Do you mean yourself?"

"I refer to everyone who works diligently every week to support themselves and their families," Ponsonby replied in a softer tone.

Sensing his displeasure at being led into giving an opinion, Mary nodded. "Though I've traveled the world and done things hardly anyone has done, particularly women, I still feel like I've led such a sheltered life. Today, I've realized how little I've really understood."

"There's no reason for Your Grace to understand," Ponsonby said. "If the time comes, and we must hope it doesn't come here, I've no doubt you will work as hard as anyone else."

"You say hope," Mary said. "Do you really think the Soviets will win this Cold War and I'll be scrubbing floors to earn my keep?"

"We must trust not, milady. I'm sure our people wouldn't go along with it. No matter how many here are found to be working for them in this country."

Mary frowned. "You don't believe this strange affair we're investigating involves the communists, do you?"

"I couldn't say, milady, but we hear such stories of the party overturning governments around the world. I would imagine King Raheem is high on their list, particularly as he's only just recovered his kingdom from them."

"That's why he's so keen to be friends with our royals and our government," Mary agreed. "After all, they weren't our friends only a few years ago."

"International relations always put me in mind of the school playground," Ponsonby said. "Stormy relationships, wild break ups, incoherent fights, and dramatic reconciliations."

Mary chuckled at the strange analogy, and her thoughts turned to her own experience. She laughed. "I had governesses, so I don't know schools, but if everything Roland told me about his school days is to be believed, you're probably right."

She sipped her sherry and relaxed her shoulders. For a moment, sadness crept into her heart at the sudden mention of her dear departed husband.

Fearing her mood would decline, she changed the subject. "Have you heard anything back from the Butlers' Club?"

"Not yet," Ponsonby said. "It's still early. A few may need time to overcome their scruples before they'll talk."

This time, he smiled, and Mary caught it before he remedied his expression.

"Have you spoken to the chief superintendent?" he asked.

"I did briefly, and he answered as I expected," Mary said. "We'll get no new information from there. The rivalries between the different branches of government are as infuriating as the factions that plague society."

11

COOK'S RECIPE FOR A SUSPECT

Lady Mary's friend Sabine from Geneva telephoned back later that day to confirm the school existed, was well-thought-of by those in the know, and was closed for the summer. Consequently, she hadn't been able to talk to anyone other than the caretaker.

"You must find the head of the school," Mary said firmly. "It's very important."

She softened when her friend assured her she was searching for the woman, but the school principal was on a hiking tour of the Carpathians and wouldn't be back in Geneva for another week. At that time, Mary would be contacted.

After catching up on some local gossip, Mary thanked her friend and encouraged her to keep trying. "After all, the woman must stay in hotels each night, and they will have telephones, even in Carpathia."

"It's behind the Iron Curtain," her friend reminded her. "They discourage telephone calls in or out of there."

Mary sighed in disappointment. *Why would this woman whose job is teaching royalty go hiking in a country where the communists are in power? Is that a clue?*

She was still mulling over this unusual setback when Ponsonby entered the room to announce dinner. Mary relayed the update from Sabine and headed to the dining room.

"The Butlers' Club hasn't much to say yet on this subject either," Ponsonby said. "The only one who admits to being in Tzatzikistan says the photo of the princess is most likely Jezebel, but he hasn't seen her in over five years."

"I hope the girls are doing better than we are," Mary said, taking her place at the table. As she sat there, staring along the long formal dining table with all of the empty chairs, she said, "From now on, Ponsonby, I'll take my meals in the drawing room. All this solitary grandeur makes me sad."

Barkley, sitting at her side, also looked sad.

"What is it?" Mary asked, noting his forlorn expression.

"His new friend has gone home for the day," Ponsonby told her, "and I wouldn't let Barkley go with him."

"This young man, our gardener spy, is quite something," Mary said. "Today was as I feared. I always knew when he was passing a window in the ballroom because the girls would be ogling him and giggling in just that way I remember all too well. When I went to meet him, I learned that Barkley is smitten too."

"I'm sorry, milady," Ponsonby said. "In his defense, I should point out he is actually a good, energetic gardener. Cook's herb garden is complete, and the flowerbeds at the front of the house are all replanted. I wouldn't have believed a secret agent could do actual work."

Mary laughed. "At least he'll have a profession to fall back on if things go wrong here on his watch, but poor Barkley. He's separated from his new love until morning."

"Cook is pleased," Ponsonby said. "Barkley isn't begging for scraps in the kitchen so often now."

"That is good news. I've been trying to get him to eat less because he's become corpulent."

At this, Barkley looked up, and Mary spied a frown.

"I'm sorry, old friend," Mary said in reply to his grave stare, "but you have become plump these past years."

She sighed. *As have I,* she thought sadly.

At Culpeper House, Lady Mary sipped her evening nightcap and waited to hear what Ponsonby had come, in his most stately fashion, to say. Barkley lay beside the fire, his little legs running while he snored quietly in his sleep.

"Cook would like a word, milady," he said in his most superior of voices.

"Have I done something to upset her?" Mary asked, sharing a mischievous smile over the rim of her glass.

"No, milady. Of course not. Cook feels she knows who is behind the murders."

"Did she say who she thought it was?" Mary asked.

"No. I'm not sufficiently important to hear the final solution of her deliberations. I only have the pleasure of tasting her experimental sauces. Of course, if my gagging means a better sauce is created for you, Lady Mary, it is my honor."

"You have heard the preamble, I suppose," Mary queried.

"I have, milady. I was not appropriately receptive to the reasoning behind the story, and she chased me out of the kitchen with the rolling pin, which is not how good staff should conduct themselves in a society household."

Mary just about spit out her sherry as she laughed. She wiped her chin discreetly. *Something about this case, or this house, has Ponsonby in rare form. Cook too.*

It was comical how her two most devoted retainers often rubbed each other the wrong way, and *she* was called on to smooth things down.

"Please, tell Cook I'm free," Mary replied. "To be fair, at this point, none of us have any solutions that would warrant ignoring a new one."

"Very well, milady."

Ponsonby left the room in a manner that suggested he'd done all he could to dissuade her from a rash action and now she must fend for herself. She took a deep breath and sat up straight, commanding herself to be calm.

Cook, with her curly red hair untidy beneath her cap and flour on her apron, entered the room with a flounce that would have made a princess proud. It made Mary smile inside as she worked hard to maintain her poise. Cook's battles with Ponsonby always led to high emotion. If she didn't know any better, she might have thought Cook took a shine to Ponsonby.

"Ponsonby says you believe you've solved our puzzle," Mary addressed her professionally.

"I have," Cook said, her expression triumphant.

"Please sit down and tell me," Mary said, gesturing to the armchair opposite her.

Cook was as shocked as Mary could wish. "That would be unseemly, milady," she said.

"It's 1958," Mary said, "a new world where shocking things are ordinary now."

Cook shook her head. "If it's all the same to you, madam, I'll stand."

Mary smiled. "Very well. Who is our murderer?"

"That common, plain one," Cook said. "Louise Coalthorpe. Coal by name and by nature, those folks."

"Now, Cook," Mary said, "we can't dismiss people because we don't like their name or their honest hard-working profession."

"It's not her name," Cook said indignantly. "It's what her father did to climb out of the muck. If you don't mind me saying."

Mary bit her tongue. Cook was a good deal too fond of plain speaking when she was riled up.

Calmly, Mary asked, "What did he do?"

"You must know," Cook said, shocked. "He was a war profiteer. His factories made munitions in the war. He made a fortune while my nephew lost his life."

"Mr. Coalthorpe is not to blame for your family's loss, Cook," Mary said, "and surely, we needed munitions to win the war."

"We did, but they shouldn't have grown rich on the sales when the rest of us got nothing or worse."

"I understand your position," Mary said, "but their money being made from munitions doesn't make them a suspect in our murders."

"You think not?" Cook cried out and quickly stepped back as if to take back her outburst. "Well, let me tell you what I learned from *their* cook."

"*Their* cook?" Mary said.

"Yes, *their* cook," Cook said, too excited to waste time on formalities. "She was cook to a duke before these people and knows about what's proper and correct and what's not."

Mary groaned inwardly. A cook who was working beneath herself, in her own opinion, was unlikely to be an unbiased witness. Nevertheless, she answered calmly, "Very well. What does she say?"

"She says the old man is a communist," Cook said bluntly and nodded as if to further solidify her point.

"Mr. Coalthorpe?" Mary asked.

"Not him," Cook said, still agitated. "He's as smarmy and grasping as all that sort are. No, his father. He was a miner and is violently against the government and the Crown. He's angry his granddaughter is taking part in the ball and quarrels with his son about it."

Mary thought quickly. It was possible, of course, but unlikely the older man would kill people and ruin his family's good fortune.

"But your friend has no actual evidence the man has done anything wrong?" Mary asked.

"She says he goes out at night. He's a member of the Soviet Club and brings home leaflets about ending the monarchy."

"His actions are very serious," Mary agreed. "I'll look into this further. Thank you, Cook. You've provided us with a new lead that hadn't been previously considered."

Cook left the room, her cheeks rosy and her grin a mile wide.

The door closed, and Mary smiled to herself mischievously. Ponsonby would be upset to learn she'd given Cook's tale any credence, and yet, it could hold merit.

Mary wasn't acquainted with the Coalthorpes. Their post-war entrance into society was too new for her experience. She quickly made a mental list of others who would know them.

Mary was right about Ponsonby. When he arrived to take away the nightcap dishes, his manner was frosty. Even his normally blue eyes looked gray.

"We need to talk, Ponsonby," Mary said as he was preparing to leave the room.

"Your Grace?" he said imperiously.

"You were very right to have Cook tell me what she knew." Mary's words were intended to warm his frozen disposition. "However unlikely it is, we have to consider that old Mr. Coalthorpe may indeed be behind these outrages."

He made the slightest twitch in posture as he unbent a little. Mary kept her face straight so as not to allow him to catch on to her observation.

"I thought it best you know, milady, though I was inclined to dismiss it as idle gossip. It is, as you say, unlikely."

Mary nodded. "So much about this affair is unlikely, isn't it? A princess who must be a princess but behaves like an imposter for example. A death that might be accidental but may not be. A random murder of a wealthy woman in a quiet London park for no sensible reason. Another random attack on another elderly woman, me, that had no discernible motive. It's all just conjecture and happenstance. There's no sense in any of it."

"Yes milady," Ponsonby said, "but the Coalthorpes aren't the only shady family on the list of invitees."

Mary held back her grin at Ponsonby's choice of phrase, but she knew exactly who he was referring to. "You mean the Chevallier girl," Mary said.

"I do indeed. Her family has been a plague on good society since they arrived here in 1790, when the Revolutionaries were guillotining their French peers. I wonder why the Chevalliers fled. They would have been perfect Revolutionaries."

Mary laughed. "They have been rather wild through the years, though Yvonne is a lovely girl, shy even. Unlike her father, I should say."

"Perhaps, milady, though she's not *shy* so much as *reserved*. She watches people in a way that is disconcerting, and, as I say, her curtness to the other girls has been more than just awkward."

"I still think it unlikely the girl has anything to do with what's happened. She's barely out of school. Her father, now, he's a different matter altogether," Mary replied

"But it's her father I'm thinking of," Ponsonby said, "and are we sure the child isn't just clever enough to hide her true nature?"

"What motive could they have?" Mary wondered aloud.

"Her father was one of those confined during the war for being a German sympathizer," Ponsonby reminded her. "Society may have forgiven him, but has he forgiven *Society*?"

Mary frowned. "Would he put his own daughter at risk, though?"

"Maybe she's happy to be part of the plot."

"But what is the plot?" Mary asked seriously. The frustration in her voice was so obvious that Barkley cocked his head up at his mistress's discontent.

"That I don't yet know, milady, any more than I know why an elderly man, who was once a coal miner and who dislikes the monarchy, would kill people associated with a ball to which his granddaughter was invited."

"I take your point," Mary said. "Many people have old grievances, but that doesn't mean they would work out those frustrations on innocent women organizing a ball."

Ponsonby inclined his head. Mary spied his triumph. He'd defrosted. His eyes even looked like their natural cornflower blue. He was pleased to have scored a point over Cook.

"We shall proceed with caution," Mary said. "Tomorrow, we'll also alert the sleuths who have these two girls on their list to dig deeper."

MARY WAITED while Yvonne Chevallier entered the hall, removed her gloves, hat, and coat, and handed them to Ponsonby. Mary made a mental note to have Cook help them on with their coats at the end. That way, Mary would get a better sense of the women's behavior toward staff. Ponsonby was too stern a figure to bring out their worst natures. To Mary, nothing was amiss in the behavior of her guest or her butler.

"Yvonne," Mary said, stepping forward to greet her pupil. "I hope your parents are both well? I've had so little time to talk with you and no opportunity to remake old acquaintances."

"They both are very well, thank you for asking," Yvonne replied in a polite but flat tone. "They speak of you sometimes and the old days when you were all enjoying happier times."

"Yes, they were happier times," Mary said, nodding. "Too much sadness has happened since, but we must forget all that and look only to the future." When Yvonne had gone on to join the others, Mary said to Ponsonby, "When they leave, I will watch again."

At the end of the afternoon practice, having focused on precisely how to speak to the Queen, Mary's long skirt got caught up on her way to the small room across the hall, but she didn't let the ripped taffeta slow her down.

The room she had chosen to spy from had no discernable purpose but was useful for snooping on guests for it looked straight across the hall, taking in the door and cloakroom. She picked at the tear in her skirt as she looked on, wondering if this was not the room's purpose all along. After all, it would have been easy to hide peepholes among the carved paneling that covered the wall beside the room's door.

Did they have camera obscura then? She seemed to remember they did. If so, maybe the whole room was the camera's body. The house was built in dangerous times, the 1760s. Maybe watching your guests arrive was a societal norm back then.

Gaggles of girls, heads together, chattering about events they were about to attend, made their way out of the ballroom across the entrance hall.

12

THEATRICAL PERFORMANCES

The last group to leave was a small grouping of three of the debutantes—Yvonne Chevallier and two others. They were the oldest of all the girls, and their talk was of smoking, drinking, and parties. Even in class, they kept to themselves, snubbing any of the other girls who made the mistake of speaking to them.

Mary had suggested "shyness" to Ponsonby when he'd mentioned her "reserved nature," but now she got the picture that it was neither. They behaved as though they really were above the others.

Despite Mary's encouragement, Cook had been unhappy helping the princess and her friends with their coats. After all, it wasn't in her purview, but Mary saw at once that Cook was truly frightened assisting these three. Cook's hands were shaking as she assisted Yvonne into her coat. Mary wished she'd learned of this earlier, for clearly there had been earlier incidents of unpleasantness to bring Cook to this state. Deciding to ensure nothing happened today, Mary stepped out from her place behind the door and strode across the hall to take leave of the departing students. The look of relief on Cook's face was enough to convince Mary she'd done the right thing.

Arriving behind the unsuspecting young ladies, she said, "Until tomorrow, ladies, when you'll find having gentlemen of your own age for partners will help the dance tutorials go better."

"I prefer older men," Yvonne replied coldly over her shoulder as she walked out the door. "Men of our age are still boys."

Her two friends looked uncomfortable but stammered a curt "bye" before hurrying after Yvonne.

There was only one car left waiting, the chauffeur holding open the rear door. The three young women entered, and the chauffeur closed the door, nodding to Mary before slipping in behind the wheel and driving away.

Angry at the curt dismissal of her friendly overture, Mary turned away as Ponsonby closed the front door. "I hope it's them we're looking for," Mary said.

"It would be extremely satisfying, milady," Ponsonby replied.

She was about to reply when she saw Cook disappearing along a corridor leading to the back of the house.

"Cook," Mary called.

Cook returned and quietly waited to hear what was wanted of her.

"Come with me, my dear," Mary said, ushering her into the morning room. "Now," Mary said as she closed the door, "tell me about that Chevallier woman."

"I don't know as I should, your ladyship," Cook said. "It's not my place."

Recognizing the dilemma, Mary said, "I understand, but I need to know who and what I'm dealing with. You know something horrible is happening around the ball. It's possible, though I don't know how, that woman is part of it. Won't you help me find out?"

Cook frowned, torn between wanting to help and the natural caution that employees have of their employers.

"All I can tell you," Cook finally said, "is she and her two friends are not very nice toward people like me. I don't know how that helps."

Mary commented, "I'll be sure to notice them all arriving and leaving from now on. I thought my role was ensuring young ladies were ready to meet the Queen, not to teach them manners to the world in general."

Emboldened, Cook said, "That princess isn't nice either."

"Maybe she's just not familiar with our ways," Mary said, "if this is her first visit to England."

"It can't be," Cook said thoughtfully. "I've heard her telling her friends things that she could only have learned here."

"Such as?"

"She mentioned a show at the Poplar Theater that was last year," Cook said. "I only know about it because my sister lives in Poplar. Nobody outside Poplar knows that theater, and nobody would know what show was on unless they were there. It isn't exactly the West End."

"That is strange," Mary agreed. "Was there more?"

Cook shook her head. "No. When she realized I was in the cloakroom, she changed the subject."

Mary thanked Cook and let her return to her duties while she thought about this revelation. Would it be possible for the girls at that expensive Swiss school to fly to London and enjoy city life without the school noticing they were missing? She thought not. Then how? Perhaps the chief superintendent could explain it.

Griffiths, however, was out on a case, she was told when she telephoned his office. She left a message and rang for Ponsonby.

"Did Cook tell you about Jezebel's possible trip to London last year?" Mary asked when he entered the room.

"She has now," Ponsonby said. "We need to know more about that young woman's background and her travels."

"We must cast our net wider," Mary said, "and I'll bully my Geneva friend harder. No one admits to knowing anything, which is, in itself, suspicious."

"Not necessarily, milady," Ponsonby said. "If she was brought up strictly at home in a traditional way, as so often happens, and has only been allowed out under close supervision to very specific places in the West, no one will know anything about her."

Mary sighed. "I agree, but it is frustrating to know so little about such a public figure."

"She's not a public figure here, though," Ponsonby said.

"These new foreign royals are hard to place," Mary said seriously. "They come and go for one thing, particularly in the Middle East. A very unstable sort of place, I believe."

"Yes, milady," Ponsonby replied. His manner suggested it wasn't a topic he intended to speculate on.

"Do you have any ideas?" Mary asked. "Any thoughts on the princess? I know you share the opinion that she's not right, but what is an alternate explanation?"

"I couldn't say, milady. It's so odd. We may be too focused on the princess and missing the obvious with one of the others. If it wasn't for the deaths, I would surmise this was a prank, someone who wanted to ruin the preparations for the ball."

"Something else is odd," Mary said. "Do you remember last November and my visit to our local theater in Norwich?"

"A very unpleasant experience as I recall, milady."

Mary nodded. She'd received an invitation to attend from a neighbor, only to find she, herself, was the "star" of the show. The neighbor, it turned out, was an investor in the touring show, and he'd assiduously spread the word how the Duchess of Snodsbury loved the show so much she was coming out of her hermit-like state to see it. Half the county had been in the theater that night, all ogling Mary to see if she was the broken-down recluse in widow's weeds they'd all heard she'd become. She'd spent three uncomfortable hours, her mind in turmoil, barely hearing or seeing anything of the performance.

"The money and entertainment industries attract the worst kinds of people," Mary said as the feelings of that evening returned and her anger rose.

"Indeed, milady," Ponsonby said. "Sadly, they have too much influence everywhere now."

Mary nodded thoughtfully. "Is it another odd coincidence, do you think?"

"That Cook should have heard the princess talking about the theater last year and you attended for the one and only time in about a quarter of a century last year?"

"Exactly that," Mary said.

"These things happen all the time, milady. We hear something, and it reminds us of something we did that's similar," Ponsonby said.

"You're right, of course," Mary agreed. "I'm imagining things."

That evening, after the debutantes were gone and Mary was relaxing with the latest Aldous Huxley novel, *Brave New World Revisited*, she found her mind wandering away from Huxley's dark vision of the future to the equally dark vision of the events surrounding the debutante ball. She'd chosen the book because she had strong memories of Huxley and the others of those halcyon days between the wars when the earlier edition of *Brave New World* had been published. Now it was she who would have dark visions of the future if she didn't work out why people were being killed around the ball and stop it before she became next.

She pulled on the old bell cord that would summon her butler from his den.

"Ponsonby," she said when he entered the room, "we need to put our heads together right now."

"Yes, milady," he replied in that measured way she knew meant she'd disturbed him from whatever it was he did in the evenings when the house was quiet.

"Sit, and tell me frankly what your impression is of Princess Jezebel."

"It's not my place," Ponsonby said seriously, though he took the seat she'd invited him to.

"Fiddlesticks," Mary said, reminding herself of her mother who used the word whenever her children did or said something she wasn't happy with. "I've been attacked once, and I want to know if it will happen again."

"There's no evidence the princess was involved in that," Ponsonby said.

"But there's an amazing coincidence over Mrs. Bamford's death," Mary said. "That was almost certainly related to her, even if she didn't make it happen."

"Again," Ponsonby said, "she could be entirely innocent. She may simply have told someone, her father even, of the planned meeting, not realizing what it would mean if the knowledge fell into the wrong hands."

"I know all this," Mary said. "What I want is your opinion of her. Is she a princess?"

"I don't know," Ponsonby said. "To be truthful, few of these young ladies act like I'd expect a young lady to act, but then I'm no longer involved with families of quality and times have moved on. Our own Queen worked as a motor mechanic in the war only fifteen years ago. How could I say what a real princess is like in 1958?"

Mary laughed, a large smile on her face. "Yes, Ponsonby, I sometimes feel it is beneath you to serve me and others like me."

It was true. After all, when she had been a young woman, so many of her friends of the time were considered little better than trollops by the Victorian generation that was their parents. They weren't, of course, or at least she hadn't been. Roland had been the love of her life, and no one could have persuaded her to be unfaithful, but others... Well, there were stories.

"I don't feel that way at all, milady," Ponsonby said seriously, "and I would never suggest such a thing."

Realizing her teasing had truly offended, Mary said, "It's all right. I didn't mean we'd gone completely to the dogs, just that we were wild in those days between the wars."

"My example about Her Majesty was only to illustrate how much things had changed," he continued earnestly. "Not that I thought young women, or young men, had become depraved."

Mary nodded, but the point Ponsonby made was right. They were both too out of touch with society to know what was considered princess-like behavior, even more so when she took into account Jezebel came from a part of the world she knew so little about.

She smiled. "Did we shock you when we ran wild after the First War? Be honest now."

Ponsonby hesitated then nodded. "I have to admit," he said, "the behavior at many of those parties was not to my taste. I don't approve of such goings-on and have little tolerance for drunkenness in anyone. I grew up in a Methodist Chapel household, you see."

"You stayed with us so I imagine you must have grown to accept it," Mary said.

"The late duke was very good to me during the war and again by employing me after when it was so hard to find work," Ponsonby said. "I never liked what I saw in your private lives, it's true, though I could understand the need to forget what we'd all been through, and I never saw anything in your or the duke's behavior that was anything other than high spirits. If I had, it might have been different. For the rest, none of that mattered to me. I owed the Duke, and I stayed."

"My husband owed you his life, as he often said," Mary said wistfully. "The loyalty was mutual each way."

"It's kind of you to say so, milady," Ponsonby replied. "I wouldn't have said any of this, but I sensed, after having criticized the way you lived, I should explain myself more."

"I now wish we'd lived more soberly too," Mary said, a frown crossing her face. "I never lose the feeling it was that lifestyle that weakened him and left him unable to fight off the disease when it came."

"None of us can know the future, milady," Ponsonby said, "and there was so much to forget."

"How did you forget, if not with drink and wild partying?"

"I'm not a religious man," Ponsonby said, "but my upbringing schooled me to accept adversity. We chapel goers are big on suffering in this 'vale of tears.' It gave me the strength of mind to survive even the horrors of the First War."

"I can see that," Mary said. "Unfortunately, it also makes it impossible for you to jump to conclusions about people, so I repeat my question. Is the princess real or not? And I'd like a snap judgment, not a considered one. Just 'yes' or 'no.'"

"Very well," Ponsonby said. "No."

"Good. That's my feeling also," Mary said. "Unfair as it may be for it is only a feeling, I think she's an imposter."

"We also have the reports from our assistants, milady," Ponsonby said. "They haven't finished their inquiries, but no one else comes even close to being so suspicious as the princess."

Mary nodded. "I never thought any of the others could really be a dangerous revolutionary."

"Again, our secret service thought the same about Burgess and MacLean before they fled to Moscow," Ponsonby reminded her.

"Yes, thank you," Mary said a little coldly, for she remembered many more parties before, during, and after the war, where both men had been drinking with them and all their friends.

Ponsonby's reminder was a chilling wake-up call. Traitors could be men or women next to you at any given time. Nobody could be above suspicion, not even the young women she was ensuring wouldn't do anything vulgar when they met the Queen.

"I've just thought of something," Mary said. "I wonder if part of the reason they do these classes is so the mentor—that's me— can assess if any of the debutantes hold a grudge against the Sovereign or have lunatic political beliefs."

"Were you asked to assess that?" Ponsonby asked.

"No," Mary admitted, "but it may have been expected, and until now, I never even thought of it. I was so wrapped up in my safety I never considered the Queen's."

"There'll be plenty of security at the ball, I'm sure," Ponsonby said.

"But each one of them goes up to the Queen in person," Mary pointed out, "and there'll be plenty of sharp objects in the room. There always are, and I don't mean tongues or wit."

"Do you have doubts about any of them?" Ponsonby asked.

"None," Mary said, "but we invited Burgess and MacLean to parties year in and out without spotting they were Soviet agents. You see what I mean?"

"I do indeed, milady," Ponsonby said thoughtfully. "Should

we ask the assistants to consider the people they interviewed for such leanings?"

Mary shook her head. "We can't ask it of them. They're too young to understand. They'll either say everyone is a Soviet agent because of some silly remark, or they'll say no one could be."

"Then you and I must be extra vigilant over the remaining classes, milady."

"I'll ask Eleanor if the girls have been vetted by the intelligence service. They might have been, with a foreign princess taking part." She paused and then added, "Though after what we said earlier about traitors in our midst, I have little confidence even if the security services *have* looked into their backgrounds."

"This ball has run for nearly two hundred years without trouble of that kind, milady. Our alarm is because of the two deaths that may yet prove to be coincidences."

"One coincidence, I'd accept," Mary said. "Two I can't believe. I'm going to telephone Eleanor now."

The telephone call wasn't exactly reassuring. Yes, the girls had been vetted except for the princess. They had the Tzatzikistan Royal Family and Embassy's word she wasn't mixed up in terrorist gangs. That wasn't very reassuring.

Everything came back to the princess, Mary thought ruefully as she left the telephone and returned to the drawing room.

"Well, milady?" Ponsonby asked before she reached the door. He, too, had obviously been waiting anxiously for good news.

Mary shook her head before explaining what she'd been told.

"I wish it were possible to have the princess miss this event," Ponsonby said. "She could meet the Queen on someone else's vigil, not ours."

As this was a sentiment Mary herself had been thinking, she couldn't do anything but agree with him.

"Unfortunately," she said, "we would need her to drop out, not us to be seen forcing her out."

After an hour trying to immerse herself in her book and failing, she went to bed and spent a sleepless night fantasizing ever more elaborate plans to make Jezebel quit without it appearing Mary had engineered it.

13

INTERVIEWS

The following day, Mary invited her assistants to stay behind after the class ended and report on their findings. When the sleuths were all assembled, she had Barkley and Ponsonby join them in the library, a suitable environment for serious discussion.

"I've called you here to review what we've learned and attempt to find an answer to the puzzle we have," Mary said. "We'll start with everyone giving an account of what they've learned. Then, when we all have the same understanding, we can plan our next steps. Winnie, will you start us off?"

"I will, but before I do, Lady Mary, I have to tell you the other girls have taken it badly that we are working with you."

"Very badly," Margie said. "Snooping is how they see it."

Mary raised her hand to stop Dotty interjecting and said, "When I said sleuthing was often dirty, I didn't just mean mud. People do take it badly when they're questioned about what they see is their business and no one else's."

The three were silent for a moment before Winnie continued, "I mentioned it because it likely affects what we've learned.

The girls have talked together and may have provided information that isn't entirely correct."

"I understand," Mary said, "but you'll find if you continue investigating puzzles, that people rarely tell the whole truth and nothing but the truth. We can only sift through what we have and try to get to the bottom of it."

Winnie nodded. "Then I'll begin. I've only interviewed one deb on my list so far, Daphne Sproat. She and I have never liked each other, and the interview went badly, so badly I couldn't face doing another right away."

Mary nodded sympathetically. "It can be difficult when personal feelings are against the sharing of confidences. Were you able to learn anything?"

Winnie frowned. "Nothing, but I have the impression she very much wants the ball to happen and her to be in it. Her family are bankers, you know, and will see this event as important to them. I can't believe she or her family are behind the events we're investigating. I did get some names who might speak for Daphne, though, and I'll do that tonight."

"Good," Mary said. "We must hope the animosity you mention doesn't affect our efforts."

Winnie laughed uncertainly. "I'm more concerned it doesn't affect my family. I learned after that we bank at the bank her father is the head of."

"I'm sure it won't," Mary said, though she knew such things happened. "Now, Margie, what have you learned?"

Margie smiled. "I had more success than Winnie," she said. "Two of my interviews went really well, and I can confidently say they and their families are not behind these murders." She paused, her expression growing more serious. "Then I had an experience similar to Winnie's, and I fear a long-standing feud I have with fellow deb, Ursula Mallory, has now grown worse."

"Investigating has that effect sometimes," Mary said. "How will you get around the difficulty?"

"I already have," Margie said. "Mama and Mrs. Mallory are old friends, and she says we needn't have any suspicions about the Mallory family. It seems it's only me that Ursula doesn't like, and that has nothing to do with the ball."

Mary laughed. "May we know why Ursula doesn't like you?"

Margie blushed hotly. "No," she said. "It was a long time ago, and it was stupid. That's all I'm going to say."

Shaking her head, smiling in amusement, Mary turned to Dotty. "And you, Dotty?"

"My investigations went well," Dotty said. "I have enough information on all three on my list to be confident two of them are not the problem."

"Which means, one might be," Mary suggested.

"Possibly, but I don't think so. Louise Coalthorpe, the one with the strong perfume, has an interesting family and, sadly, a personal problem."

The others sat up. This was the first hint of a clue.

"Well?" Mary asked when Dotty seemed to have drifted into one of her reveries.

"Her grandfather was a coal miner when he started the business. He's a member of the Soviet Club and hates the monarchy. He argues with Louise's father about the ball and Louise's invitation to attend," Dotty said.

"And the personal problem?"

Dotty hesitated, struggling with words. "This can't leave the room," she said, looking around at them all. When they'd agreed, she continued, "Louise has what advertisements call BO, and particularly when she becomes nervous, even deodorants don't stop it. The scent masks the problem."

Mary said thoughtfully, "Individually, these aren't strong evidence, but together, maybe they are. If her grandfather is a serious danger, then Louise, feeling shunned and excluded, may well be the weapon he needs to carry out an attack." She paused. "What's your opinion, Dotty?"

"My opinion is that the old man is like lots of old people—cranky—and Louise would like to be included too much to take part in anything like the events we've seen."

"Thank you, Dotty," Mary said. "Now, we've heard what we've learned so far. What are your thoughts? Anyone?"

"That we have no credible suspect who might be in any way responsible for the two murders other than Jezebel," Winnie said bluntly. "To be honest, we knew that at the outset."

Her two companions nodded their agreement.

"Are you sure you aren't absolving Louise Coalthorpe now just because you feel sorry for her?" Mary asked. "After all, if any of them have a strong grievance and a background that might be opposed to the aristocracy and the monarchy, it's her."

"That's true," Dotty said, "but I talked to her, and I'm convinced she'd love to be accepted. I don't feel she wants to hurt people."

"But Lady Mary is right," Winnie said. "What you took to be the anguish of being excluded through no real fault of her own may have been suppressed rage against the world and her latest rejection."

"She hasn't been rejected," Margie cried. "She's here every class and still going to the ball."

"But no one is her friend," Winnie said. "She's always either alone or on the edge of the crowd."

"Well, she should use a stronger deodorant," Margie said. "Other people do."

Dotty replied, "My brother says she does, but the moment she gets nervous, the stuff doesn't work."

"All the more reason for us to help her practice," Mary said. "We don't want her to be nervous near the Queen. A strong

Danish blue, gorgonzola, or ripe stilton is acceptable. A debutante with a dubious scent is not."

"I'm sure the thought of tripping over her gown or some other mishap as she meets the Queen terrifies her," Dotty said. "It does me, anyway."

"Then we have to work with her until she can do the whole presentation routine in her sleep without a moment's concern," Mary said. "We start tomorrow."

The three assistants looked at her, but their faces showed no dislike of the idea so Mary let it pass.

"I still think we're taking too much on trust with our wish to help," Winnie said. "Her grandfather is a socialist, and she has a problem. Dotty's good wishes are no more than that. They're not evidence of innocence."

"We can accept her innocence while keeping our eyes open," Margie said, "but I'm with Dotty on this. We should move on. None of the people we and Barkley suspected have turned out to be worth investigating further."

"We haven't found a new lead, it's true," Mary agreed, "but we haven't yet explained how the princess can be involved. She wasn't even here when Lady Hilary died."

"But she was known to be coming," Margie said. "It may not be her doing this, but it's her presence that drives the murders. We can be sure of that."

"It's disappointing no one at the Butlers' Club could add anything new," Mary said to Ponsonby. "My Geneva friend, Sabine, couldn't add anything new either."

"With the Tzatzikistan government leaning to the East these past years," Ponsonby said seriously, "the last British butler was thrown out of the country some years ago."

"And with the Geneva school closed for the summer," Mary said, "the only information I was able to retrieve was that Jezebel had been a pupil and had left for London at the end of term."

Dotty said, "I'm not interested in politics, but why did the Government of Tzatzikistan favor the East and why are they now favoring the West?"

"When King Farouk was overthrown in Egypt back in 1952," Ponsonby said, "King Raheem decided we hadn't supported Farouk as we should have. It made him turn to the Eastern bloc for help."

"But Communists hate monarchs, don't they?" Dotty asked.

"They do," Mary said, "but politics often makes for strange bedfellows. I imagine they made it worthwhile for Raheem to close off his lands and oil to us."

"He couldn't have been silly enough to believe they'd let him stay on the throne, though, could he?" Margie asked.

"Maybe he thought he could manage them, or maybe he thought he could change his title to President-for-Life, which is much the same thing," Ponsonby said, "but they didn't let him stay on. He was forced into exile for a time. Then he returned and took back control, which is why we are where we are."

"With a princess no one has seen since she was a child, being presented to the Queen," Winnie said. "You don't think the way she behaves just reflects the way people over there began behaving to satisfy their new communist friends?"

"Possibly," Mary said, "or she's just learned a lot of western ways in Switzerland, which is why it's so difficult to say she's an imposter."

"She doesn't have to be an imposter, though, does she?" Dotty said. "She could be real and have joined the revolution."

"Which revolution are we talking about?" Winnie asked.

"The revolution that's about to happen," Margie said. "Until it happens, you don't know it's going to. It's only after that you realize the signs that might have warned you."

"Very true," Mary said, impressed at the understanding her

young assistants were displaying. "Imposter or would-be revolutionary, we have nothing to say she's either."

"We have reasons to doubt her, milady," Ponsonby said, "beyond just our combined intuitions. Her behavior suggests something is amiss. The fact none of the others have a motive, so far as we can see, and we can find nothing about her, the fact no one knows her..."

"And don't forget her ankles," Mary interjected, smiling at Dotty who was about to speak. "What you say is true, Ponsonby, but we have no proof. Nothing directly points to her being a bad person."

"As Margie said, she doesn't have to be a bad person, milady," Ponsonby said. "After all, even if she's genuine and well-intentioned, her presence may still be the catalyst for the murders."

"Except," Mary said, "we can't say why. If the two women were murdered because the princess was coming, it can only mean she's an imposter, or why bother?"

Winnie frowned. "Lady Mary, just because we haven't found a reason doesn't mean a reason doesn't exist."

Mary nodded. "True, but I don't see it. The more I consider the matter, the more sure I am that she's an imposter, and if she isn't here to kill the Queen and start a war then why?" Mary paused and then cried out, "To intercept something only the princess would be given. Why didn't I see it before?"

There was silence as the group considered this.

After a moment, Ponsonby said, "I can't believe any father would put his daughter in danger carrying something dangerous from one country to another."

"But a princess would be the safest messenger," Margie said. "No one would search her or her baggage, and both would be guarded throughout the journey. Lady Mary is right. The princess was to carry something home, something that someone doesn't want carried home."

"It can't be something very big," Dotty said, "and it can't be really dangerous, not like explosives, I mean."

"Maybe it's just a message," Winnie suggested, "something she can learn and repeat when she returns home. That way, there's nothing to be carried, nothing physical, I mean."

"Then it must be a message that's too long to send by radio, where it might be intercepted by people listening in and short enough to be memorized," Mary said. "A time, place, and date, maybe."

The others shivered. It was all too plausible. An assassination plan, perhaps.

"It must be longer, milady," Ponsonby said. "We listened to German army radio in the war and wouldn't have found a message that short. It takes time for the listener to find the right frequency."

"We had to learn poetry by heart at school," Dotty said, grimacing, "and some of those were very long. I usually couldn't, but many could recite even the longest of poems after only a few days of studying."

"A plan, maybe," Winnie said. "With names, dates, times, and places. Not just one, many."

Mary nodded. "That's the sort of thing I have in mind."

"And it wouldn't matter if she's real or an imposter," Margie said. "She only has to be on the side of whoever needs this message."

"Then shouldn't we stop investigating Jezebel's background and start asking what it is she's here for?" Dotty asked.

"It also does away with the question of why the whole embassy accepts her as the princess if she's not," Ponsonby remarked. "They accept her as the princess because she is, but they don't realize she is working for revolutionaries."

"Maybe she isn't," Mary said. "It could be she's here to pick up the message, or whatever it is, but she's unaware that, once she has it, she'll be captured and made to hand it over."

"But," Winnie said, "if she's not an imposter, what was the reason for killing Lady Hilary and Mrs. Bamford?"

The group fell silent again.

After a moment, Lady Mary said, "In fact, we're no further forward, are we?"

"Beyond having eliminated the other young ladies," Ponsonby said.

Dotty raised her hand tentatively as though still back in school. "As I said, we have to concentrate on Jezebel's actions going forward. Nothing else can help us now."

"How can we do that?" Margie asked. "She's brought here from the embassy in an embassy car and returns the same way. We can't follow the car on foot or spy on the embassy all day and night, can we?"

They fell silent again. Dotty's point was a good one, but Margie's objections were very real.

"We could follow the car," Winnie said. "Mama drops me off here every day. I know she'd be happy to lie in wait at the embassy gate and follow Jezebel here and do the same when returning home. For her, it would be like the old days."

"We don't have to be spying on the embassy all day and night," Margie said. "After all, she can hardly slip out of there on her own outside of normal hours. The guards would see her, either at the gates or climbing the fence. She can only leave the embassy with an escort and during the hours when the world is awake, surely?"

"But she still may go to the theater in the evening," Mary said. "Your parents wouldn't let you sit outside the embassy alone after dark, and even if you could, you couldn't follow an embassy car taking Jezebel to an event."

"But I could," Ponsonby said. "There's little for me to do after dinner is served."

Mary considered this. "There's only me for dinner. Cook won't like it, but I could have a sandwich, and we could both spy or at least take turns."

"We could take turns during the day," Winnie said, "at least I could."

She looked at her two colleagues, who were considering how easily they could persuade their parents they were engaged in legitimate business and not hanging around street corners where their presence may be misconstrued.

"Would your mothers be happy with this?" Ponsonby asked. His expression suggested he expected mothers to be unhappy, even old sleuthing mothers.

"They did dangerous things when they were our age," Winnie replied.

"Ponsonby is suggesting that while parents might do risky things sometimes," Mary said, "they're a lot more careful when it comes to their children doing risky things."

The three young women looked at each other waiting for a decision.

"I'm game," Margie said at last. "Mama will understand."

"Me too," said Dotty, nodding in that dreamy way Mary was beginning to realize wasn't lack of sharpness, more an affectation.

"Then we need to start by reconnoitering the embassy," Ponsonby said, nodding. "There may be more than one exit, and one person may not be enough."

"We start tomorrow," Mary said, "but with the understanding that, if at any time, any of you young people feel you're in danger, you leave immediately. Is that understood?"

The three sleuths nodded.

"Are we agreed?" Mary demanded, refusing to let them remain silent.

"We agree," they said almost in unison.

"Good. Then we can close tonight's meeting," Mary said. "We will meet here at ten o'clock in the morning and begin our surveillance."

14

HIGH SPIRITS

The following morning, Mary and the girls looked out of the car window as Ponsonby drove slowly past the Tzatzikistan Embassy. It wasn't a large building but an older home in more prosperous times with added offices and garages. The property backed onto a city park with a pond and benches for people to sit on while they fed the ducks, of which there were many. The railings separating the embassy grounds from the public park were suitably ornamental but also suitably secure. There was no gate or entrance on that side.

A trade entrance on one side of the building was also well guarded by railings and a strong gate. They saw a van being allowed in by a guard stationed in a small gatehouse nearby.

"She wouldn't use the tradesmen's entrance," Winnie said with a laugh.

"The guard would report on her movements if she tried to, anyway," Margie said.

At the end of the street, Ponsonby turned the car and drove slowly back.

"Two exits," Mary said, "and both can be seen from this

point here." She pointed to a small teashop on the opposite side of the street. "This will make a good observation post."

"We'll have to drink a lot of tea," Dotty said.

"And eat a lot of scones and pastries," Margie added. "I can't afford that for too long."

"I'll pay," Mary said, adding severely, "and you will restrain yourselves from overindulging."

The girls giggled.

Mary guessed the first days might be heavy on her purse. After that, they would become sickened by it all, and the cost would reduce. She hoped so, anyway.

"We should start now," Winnie said. "I'll get out here, and someone will have to relieve me in time to be home to pick up my mother and the car for our afternoon class."

Mary asked Ponsonby to stop, and Winnie jumped out.

Mary handed her a five-pound note and said, "That has to last you more than today."

Winnie said sweetly, "Cafes in this part of town will be expensive, you can be sure."

"You forget," Mary said, "I will be watching from this cafe this evening, and I'll know then how much you've bought."

Winnie laughed and walked quickly back down the street to begin her stakeout.

"Can either of you come back to relieve her?" Mary asked Margie and Dotty.

"I can," Dotty said. "We don't live far from here. Mother and I often walk to the park behind the embassy. I never thought I'd be investigating it."

"Dress sensibly and carry your classroom clothes in a bag," Mary said. "You can change when you arrive at Culpeper House."

"I'll tell my parents I'm going to Winnie's house after class,"

Margie said. "That way, we can cover the time Jezebel returns to the embassy and you arrive to take the evening shift, Lady Mary."

⚬ ⚬ ⚬ ⚬ ⚬ 🐾 ⚬ ⚬ ⚬ ⚬ ⚬

WINNIE ORDERED a Chelsea Bun and a pot of tea the moment the cafe opened. Even though it was a bright May morning, she'd been cold while nonchalantly pacing up and down the street, trying not to look like she was monitoring the embassy.

Her vigil from the cafe, while confirming its suitability as an observation post, was tedious and without reward. By the time Dotty arrived, Winnie had eaten two Chelsea buns and ordered two more pots of tea. She groaned as her stomach swelled uncomfortably.

"Anything to report?" Dotty asked.

"Only that Lady Mary was right," Winnie said. "We should not overindulge in the delicacies."

Dotty laughed and went to the counter to order her lunch. When she returned, Winnie was already prepared to leave.

"You saw nothing?" Dotty asked again.

"Cars and vans coming and going," Winnie said, "but unless Jezebel was hidden among the dirty laundry, she didn't leave the embassy."

"In spy novels," Dotty said seriously, "that's exactly how people come and go from embassies."

"Then we're going to eat a lot of pastries for no result," Winnie said, laughing. "I think we can live with that. See you soon."

Dotty took up the chair Winnie had vacated and stared at the embassy gates across the street. Her tea and cucumber sandwiches arrived, and she nibbled and sipped slowly as the minutes slipped by. Her hope that something would happen on her lookout slowly drained away as the hours passed, and she was mightily relieved when Winnie's family car pulled up outside, and she was able to leave the cafe and jump inside.

"Anything?" Winnie asked.

"Not a sausage," Dotty said, grimacing. "Not even a laundry van."

"Now we wait," Winnie said.

They didn't have long to wait. Right on time, the embassy car, with Jezebel in the back, pulled out of the embassy gate and headed for Culpeper House.

"Follow that car," Winnie instructed the driver, who rolled his eyes while her mother smiled at such theatrics.

"I've been longing to say that all morning," Winnie said to Dotty as their car took up a position two cars back of the embassy car and threaded its way through London's afternoon traffic.

The embassy car didn't stop, much to Winnie and Dotty's disappointment. They'd really hoped they would be the ones to make the breakthrough the case needed. Both cars arrived at the entrance to Culpeper House together. As they stepped out, the two assistant sleuths smiled in what they hoped was an innocent way at Jezebel, who'd left her car and was preparing to make her grand entrance. They followed her in, conscious they weren't nearly as elegant or superior as Jezebel.

"She's an actress," Dotty said when they were inside and the chatter from the other young women would drown out her comment. "Real people don't posture and pose the way she does."

"Maybe princesses do," Winnie said, though on balance, she fancied Dotty to be right. Jezebel's manner was brittle and artificial.

"Ladies," Mary shouted, making herself heard above the hubbub of chattering students. Her voice brought them to order eventually, and she was able to continue. "Today is the day for us to meet the young gentlemen. I want you to remember, this ball is *your* event, not theirs. They will be there, I haven't invited anyone who wouldn't be, but they are secondary to the purpose of the evening—your introduction to the Queen."

She paused as she saw their expressions become grave. Maybe, for the first time, they were beginning to understand their role and why they were being asked to train for it.

Having piqued their interest, she continued, "I expect you to guide the young men today and every day after, if I'm honest, but mainly today. Do not let their levity infect you. I telephoned their mothers and asked them to impress upon their sons the seriousness of this event. However, I know they'll wish to be playful and irreverent because it's what young men do. You *must* quell this. This afternoon, we'll walk through the whole ball with all that it entails, and you have to keep them focused."

The room was now silent, and every face showed the seriousness that Mary had impressed upon them. She could only hope it would last throughout the afternoon as the boys began creating mischief.

Seeing the girls were now ready to start, Mary turned and nodded to Ponsonby who was waiting at the door. A group of self-conscious-looking young men filed in. Clearly, Ponsonby had coached them in their roles. They looked like puppies who'd had a "talking to."

They began with a simple country dance, one where couples occasionally held hands and nothing more, and all the partners moved seamlessly throughout the whole class. No one was particular to anyone, and everyone had a partner, however briefly the partners were joined.

It couldn't last, of course. As the "ball" continued, dances had more contact, and partners remained with each other throughout the whole dance. This was where Mary knew it would grow more difficult. The most desirable girls and boys would necessarily want to stick to each other, and that couldn't be allowed—not here in training nor at the ball.

Between sets, participants mingled and sipped the alcohol-free punch Ponsonby had provided. Mary was just priding herself on a successful event when she noticed a young man screening one of the punch bowls with his body as his arms appeared suspiciously active, his hands out of sight. She walked quickly to the door, where Ponsonby hovered just outside.

"Center punch bowl," Mary whispered. "It may have just been adulterated with alcohol. Have it removed."

Ponsonby nodded and strode quickly around the room to the table with the suspected punch bowl. He gestured to Cook, who was waiting for emergencies to occur. She took the bowl and hurried away, while Ponsonby, keeping one eye firmly on the remaining bowls, followed to open the door for her exit. It wasn't long before Cook returned with a re-filled bowl.

"Quickly as you can, Cook. The other bowls are almost empty," Ponsonby said.

All eyes in the room followed Cook's progress across the room. Mary smiled to herself. Everyone was in on this, she now knew. For all their innocent expressions, they were teenagers after all.

The music began again, and Mary was pleased to witness the disappointed pupils and guests being drawn back to following the dance master's direction.

However, as the dancing continued, Mary saw the expressions slowly changing. She saw quick grins exchanged, winks, smirking smiles that couldn't be suppressed, and she knew. Spiking the punch bowl was a trick to divert her attention. The real danger lay elsewhere.

Trying not to make her search obvious, she scanned the room and the dancers for clues. Should she remove all the fruit punch bowls? She viewed the dancers, hoping to spot eyes drawn to the tables where the harmless fruit drinks were placed, but she saw none. Not the punch bowls, she decided.

The snacks hadn't been brought into the room, so *they* were safe. What did that leave? Only the dancers themselves. What could they do? They were planning something. Many of the girls were openly giggling, and the boys were trying to maintain their stiff upper lips and failing miserably.

The music stopped, and a young man near the record player said, "I'll change it."

The dance master, who'd wandered away from the machine, nodded agreement.

A moment later, Mary and the dance master were surprised to hear a young man's voice singing, almost shouting, about a hound dog crying and the room filled with dancers jitterbugging or something very like it.

Mary remembered the jitterbug from wartime events. It led to dancers perspiring, ladies showing too much leg, and, later, everyone behaving in ways that weren't at all seemly. Mary approved of all these things for young people, just not here and not now. She was still weighing her options—let it continue to encourage conviviality or stop it—when Barkley decided for her.

He was as excited as the humans. Running into the crowd, he caused pandemonium. Every couple he approached tried to include or avoid him. It made no difference what they tried. He got under their feet, and down one partner or the other would go, landing with a thump on their behinds, letting out high-pitched screams of laughter or outrage.

Mary quickly signaled to the dance master to shut the music off. He did so, and the wild dancing slowly stopped, although the laughter didn't for some time. Barkley, looking as disappointed as the young people, trotted back to Mary's side. She scolded him, and he did his best to look penitent, but his demeanor suggested he considered the laughter as appreciative applause.

The dance master lifted the small disk from the turntable with his fingertips. It was one of those 45 RPM things that looked like they were intended for drink coasters from the moment they were made. He replaced it with a large 78 RPM record. This exchange was significant, replacing the new flimsy throwaway music with a return to that which was old, solid, and real.

When silence settled in the room, Mary signaled the dance master to resume the lesson. The less said about this the better, she thought.

The music he put on, and the dance it involved, a lively Gay Gordons, at least allowed the young people to burn off some of their energy in the way a waltz could not.

At the break for refreshments, Mary asked Winnie, "Was that one of Elvis Presley's recordings?"

"It was," Winnie said, adding excitedly, "Isn't he great?"

Mary smiled as memories of jitterbugging the night away in wartime clubs and parties flickered, like moths in candlelight, through her mind. She nodded. "I expect I'd think so, if I were your age," she said wistfully.

"Is something bothering you about this song, Lady Mary?" Winnie asked.

"It was a line I heard, I didn't like," Mary said. "Something about the girl being thought of as 'high class' but not being so. Doesn't that strike you as exactly our feelings about the princess?"

"Oh, Lord," Winnie said. "I never considered that. Do you think she will know we were hinting at her?"

"If she does," Mary replied, "she can't say it, because then we'd know she really is an imposter. No, but it led me to thinking about some of the others. Miss Coalthorpe, for example."

Winnie groaned. "I never thought of that either." She looked across at the others. "She doesn't appear to be upset. Maybe she didn't notice."

"We must hope not."

"I'm sure no one thought of it when the idea was being talked of," Winnie said.

"It would be very wrong if it had been," Mary said grimly. She shrugged in a most unladylike fashion. "I suppose it's just one of those awful coincidences that happen in life where harmless people are hurt when no hurt was intended."

"It is," Winnie said. "The record isn't even one of ours. It belongs to Johnny Cadbury's older brother. He brought it back from a trip to America."

"And you all thought something so exotic would liven up our stuffy class?"

"Well, yes," Winnie said, smiling mischievously. "You have to admit all this training is a bit over the top. We're all schooled in this from the age of ten, and we receive at most thirty seconds with the Queen."

Mary nodded. "I agree," she said, "and if I'm involved with it next year, there'll be a lot fewer classes. I don't wish to speak ill of the dead, but Lady Hilary seems to have thought you were orphans taken from the streets."

Winnie laughed. "She was an old fusspot, but she always meant well. She was a gentle soul too. What happened to her was wrong."

"We aren't really sure she was murdered," Mary said. "The scientists are still arguing."

"Humph. So says the police," Winnie replied. "But getting back to the earlier topic, you definitely don't think we should talk to Louise Coalthorpe to be sure she isn't offended by it?"

"When you all discussed this foolish prank," Mary said, "was she there?"

"No, she's not really one of the group," Winnie said.

"Pity. Well, she shows no sign of agitation or anger, so we shouldn't make any more of it than it is. Perhaps she couldn't understand it. After all, it wasn't exactly standard English."

"There are others who also might feel injured," Winnie said, examining all the other students who might consider that it was aimed at them.

"Everyone saw it as a prank against me and not a dig at them, so we'll leave it like that. If the matter comes up later, we'll deal with it then. Now, the break is over. Swing back to that young man you were dancing with before someone snatches him away."

"They can't," Winnie said gaily. "We're practically engaged." With that, she walked quickly away.

Mary sighed and shook her head. The gap between "practically" and "actually" was a wide one, and she knew many couples that had fallen into it over the years.

Sensing something was wrong, Mary surveyed the room. Immediately, she saw the problem. There were couples missing.

She clapped her hands as she walked nearer the dancers. "Who is missing?" she demanded, to a chorus of laughter.

Mary glared at Winnie, whose shocked expression suggested

she didn't know anything about this new prank. Mary turned her gaze to Margie, who looked equally surprised, and then Dotty, whose eyes flicked toward the French windows that were opened out onto the terrace.

Mary hurried to the doors and stepped out into the warm afternoon sunshine. Her missing dancers weren't on the terrace. She scurried along the terrace to the corner of the house. Rounding the corner, she found one couple enjoying a smoke.

"Where are the others?" she demanded.

The two laughed and pointed to an open door farther along the side of the house.

"Finish those cigarettes," Mary said severely, "and return to the ballroom." When they appeared to hesitate, she added, "Now!"

It wasn't often Mary became angry, but this nonsense was beyond a joke.

Unconcerned, the couple sauntered back toward the ballroom, stubbing out their cigarettes with their feet as they went.

Mary was torn between following them back, sure that the other couple would already be back in the ballroom, pretending they'd never left, and going on to the open door to chase them down in case they'd found their way into some other part of the house for even less socially acceptable behavior. Finally, she decided to follow the first couple back to the ballroom and was relieved to discover she'd guessed right. There were now the full complement of couples.

She waved to the dance master to begin the remainder of the lesson while she took deep breaths to calm herself. These were just silly pranks, but she was responsible for the young people while they were here. Should word of these pranks slip out, she could forget being invited back next year. Worse, the fathers of those two girls may well be angry that the girls had been allowed to wander off privately with young men. Fathers tended to be protective of their daughters, as she remembered from her own youth. She doubted things had changed that much in the intervening years.

When Ponsonby entered the room with Cook to clear away the refreshments, she drew him aside and asked if he'd seen a couple alone in the house.

"I did, milady," he replied, "and escorted them here before they could disappear."

"There's only one more week, then we will be done with it," Mary said. "I want all those terrace doors locked the whole time."

Ponsonby nodded gravely. "It will be done. There will be no young men in those last classes, will there?"

"No. It's just a recap of everything we've gone through with the girls," Mary said. "Nevertheless, I'm not leaving anything to chance."

"We must have Barkley inspect them as they arrive, in case they bring anything in with them."

"And I need to greet everyone," Mary said, "and you inspect them as they pass through the hall."

"Frisk them, as they say in the movies," Ponsonby said.

"Well, not quite that," Mary replied, unsure if he was joking or not.

One could never tell with butlers. Their straight faces were beyond inscrutable.

"Cook," Mary said, for she was about to leave the room with a trolley of dishes, "you need to be aware that our young ladies may be plotting more mischief in the last classes. We all need to scrutinize them closely when they arrive, particularly when you take their coats, hats, and gloves. You might observe things we miss."

"Very well, milady," Cook said, "though I hope there'll be

nothing for me to report, my eyes not being what they used to be, and spying on people isn't my way."

After assuring Cook she understood her feelings, Mary turned her attention back to the class, which she now viewed with a jaundiced eye. They looked back with guilty expressions, which mollified her a little.

15

THE UNWANTED GIFT

The next day, Princess Jezebel entered the ballroom with her usual haughty swagger. It was the swagger of a triumphant adult, not the superior grace of a noble youngster. Mary frowned. Her whole being rebelled against this young woman being a princess, new or old, eastern or western. Then, she saw the brooch.

"What a lovely brooch, Jezebel," Mary said, catching her eye.

Jezebel smiled and nodded. Even the smile wasn't the smile of a girl proud of a new possession. It was... Mary couldn't put her finger on it.

"Is it from an admirer?" Mary asked as Jezebel was showing no sign of explaining.

Jezebel laughed. "Not exactly," she said. "More of an old goat."

Again, she stopped, which frustrated Mary even more.

"I don't understand," Mary said. "If you don't like the person, why did you accept his gift?"

Jezebel shrugged. "He's an old friend of my father's from back in the Dark Ages of our country. He's lived in London forever, but he and father are still in touch. I suppose he thought giving me this would raise his standing in father's eyes."

"A diplomatic gift," Mary said, smiling. "Well, you are here to be an ambassador."

Jezebel nodded. "That's why I accepted the gift. It's hideous, really, so old-fashioned no one but an old sultana could like it."

"The gift is very nice," Mary said, though she understood the girl's objection. It looked like an old scarab brooch of the kind that was fashionable after Carter opened Tutankhamen's tomb. "They were popular when I was younger."

"Well, Lady Mary," Jezebel said, smiling sweetly, something she never did before, "you see then I am right."

"I do indeed," Mary said. "It is perhaps too big for modern tastes."

"I shall give it away," Jezebel said. "Maybe you would like it?"

"Oh, no, dear. I can't take it," Mary said, "and you can't do that. Your father's friend will have told your father of the gift. He would be devastated to learn you didn't value it."

Jezebel shrugged. "I'll say I lost it. What's it to him or my father? The brooch was given to me."

"Yes, but a diplomatic gift can't be treated like a personal gift," Mary said, shocked. "Trouble comes from insults of that kind."

"He's an old man," Jezebel replied off-handedly. "He'll be dead before I make it home, I shouldn't wonder."

Tiring of the conversation, she passed on to meet the small circle of friends she'd made among the debutantes.

Mary and Ponsonby continued greeting each student, doing their best to appear natural while trying to scan coats and hats for evidence of possible mischief. Mary glanced to see how Cook was managing and was horrified to see her staring intently at each girl and practically feeling the pockets of each coat. The students seemed oblivious and walked on without comment.

Mary took the opportunity of the brief time between two arrivals to quietly speak to Cook, suggesting she be less obvious.

Cook was puzzled. "I don't understand, milady."

"You are looking too closely and might give the game away," Mary said.

Cook reddened. "I always look closely," she said. "Otherwise, I can't connect the coat to the owner. I have done nothing different today."

The explanation for the girls' lack of offense became clear to Mary. Cook didn't like wearing her spectacles in public, and that small vanity the girls understood. Mary smiled and returned to her post.

As the afternoon wore on, and despite her close involvement with the girls' deportment, the conversation with Jezebel began to worry Mary. When Ponsonby and Cook brought in refreshments, she motioned Ponsonby to meet her outside the ballroom.

Once Ponsonby left the room, she signaled her assistants over to her and asked them to prepare the room and the girls for dancing with the dance master, who had just arrived. Mary welcomed him at the ballroom door before slipping out into the hall.

Ponsonby had understood her signals perfectly and was ready to hear his new orders.

"I want you to call DCS Griffiths," Mary said. "We may have something the secret service needs to know of." She briefly explained.

"What if he isn't immediately available?" Ponsonby asked. "And what shall I tell him? He will need convincing to take such a step."

Mary was well aware of the professional rivalries between the regular police, the Special Branch, and the secret service to understand where Ponsonby's question was coming from.

"That's the trouble," Mary said, frowning. "They will reason that it's just a woman's foible, on my part and Jezebel's." She paused, considering the words to impress those shady men behind the scene. There were none. It was her hunch and no more than that. "Tell him the princess has been given a gift of a brooch and she's planning to give it away. There may be something here we should stop. I don't know what, but it's odd. Giving away an expensive gift from someone she says is an old family friend."

"Very ungracious behavior," Ponsonby said gravely. "But as we've seen, she isn't gracious in anything she does."

"I know, which is why I'm afraid the authorities won't act to stop the handover," Mary said. "I feel it really is a handover."

"But why do it here or on her way back to the embassy?" Ponsonby asked thoughtfully.

"Because the authorities tightened all contacts between her and others after our last warning to them," Mary said. "This is free time, and that's why she brought it here and told me her intention. To make it look innocent."

Ponsonby nodded. "I'll call Griffiths immediately, milady, but I fear this means her contact is here in this building, for they would never stop the car going to or from the embassy."

Mary said, "Oh, Lord, I never thought of that. Are there any strangers in the house? Tradesmen, for instance?"

"None that I know of, milady," Ponsonby said, "but I'll have our MI5 'gardener' do some snooping while I telephone Griffiths." He paused, realizing what he'd just said. "Milady, the MI5 man *is* the new person in our household."

Mary, too, had realized that when he first spoke. "It can't be him, though. We have to trust he is on our side, or we're lost."

"Very well, milady," Ponsonby said, hurrying off, as anxious as she was to stop this possible handover.

But handover of what? What could be so valuable but so

small? The brooch was large, but it wouldn't hide anything much bigger than a gold Guinea coin. She returned to her pupils much perplexed.

When the class was over and her pupils were leaving, Mary went immediately to find Ponsonby.

"Did you speak to him?" Mary demanded.

"I did, milady."

"And?" There were times Mary wanted to wring Ponsonby's neck when he did his silent *'ask me questions and I'll answer them'* routine.

"He feels this isn't a lot to go on, and while he accepts Your Grace's instinct, he feels others may not. He will certainly have his constable watch the princess closely and, if she hands over the brooch, follow that person."

"Then we must observe her from the ballroom until she gets into the car," Mary said firmly. "I want to see that brooch right up until her handlers have her."

"I also advised the MI5 man he should travel back to the embassy with the princess," Ponsonby said.

"You did right. I only hope it won't alert her to our suspicions. But wait," she cried. "That might be her chance to hand it over to him, if he's the contact."

"We must hope then he isn't, milady," Ponsonby said. "As you said."

"Her driver and bodyguard would see and stop them," Mary said with relief. "Not everyone can be in on it, whatever it is."

"Quite so," he said. "Now, we're quite out of the way here, so you may also watch how the Chevallier woman treats Cook, who is waiting to hand her her coat."

Mary turned in time to glimpse exactly what Ponsonby meant. Yvonne Chevallier stood waiting while Cook tried to help her on with her coat. Words were spoken, too quiet for

Mary to hear but clearly upsetting to Cook, who became strangely nervous and awkward, a painful scene to view in an elderly woman so normally fearless.

Mary frowned. "Who has the Chevallier woman on their list?"

"The Honorable Margery," Ponsonby said.

"Then I must speak to Margie before she goes. I want to know more about that young woman before I give her a piece of my mind."

Ponsonby coughed discreetly, and Mary turned. Jezebel was leaving the ballroom with two other girls, who'd become fixtures at her side, in tow.

"I also want special attention paid to those two," Mary said, gesturing to Jezebel's companions. "Inform whoever has them."

"Certainly, milady," Ponsonby said then added in a low voice, "She still has the brooch."

Mary had seen that too. "Then I shall walk her out," she said, walking quickly across the hallway to intercept Jezebel.

"Jezebel," Mary said, catching the princess's attention. "I do hope you will reconsider your determination to give away the brooch, at least until your father knows of its existence and your reasons for giving it away."

Jezebel laughed and twisted the brooch up to the light. "Look at it," she said. "No one who sees it could have any doubts why I gave it away."

Mary did look at it. It was a deep maroon with embroidered patterns resembling Arabic writing in golden thread on it. Was it the embroidery that was the message? It was a short message if it was.

"Perhaps," she replied, "but it meant something to the giver, and if he's your father's friend, that has to count for something. Maybe even mean something."

"Very well," Jezebel said, "but will you not keep it for me? I don't want it."

"I can't. Everybody at the embassy would see it gone," Mary said. "This is your burden, and you must guard it until you understand why this was given to you. If the old man didn't tell you, perhaps your father will. Telephone him and ask?"

"I wish I could," Jezebel said gloomily as they passed out through the door to her car, where a uniformed chauffeur was holding open the door. Jezebel stepped inside and smiled sadly at Mary. The door closed.

Before the chauffeur could take his seat, the MI5 man took the front passenger seat—and Barkley jumped in with him.

Jezebel immediately jumped out of the back seat, her face furious, and her bodyguard followed her.

"Remove that dog," she shouted at Mary, who was at the door watching with great amusement.

Barkley, however, was determined to go home with his friend the gardener and crouched down between the front seats to make himself immoveable.

The driver attempted to push Barkley out, and Barkley growled and bared his teeth. The driver also leapt out of the car, furiously complaining about the intrusion.

The MI5 man grinned and cajoled Barkley, urging him to leave, but even he was unable to persuade Barkley to move. Giving up, the MI5 man unwillingly left the car also.

Barkley, realizing his friend might not be going away in the car, wriggled his way out from the seats and leapt out of the car to join his friend. Mary pounced and lifted him to her bosom.

"Bad dog, Barkley," she said while secretly scratching his belly. It had been quite a performance.

After they'd calmed down, Jezebel, the driver, and the MI5 man jumped in the car and slammed the doors. While an animated discussion went on in the car, it moved away, and a constable on a bicycle who'd been waiting at the side of the house immediately set out behind them.

"Will he be able to keep up, do you think?" Mary asked Ponsonby.

"At this time of the afternoon, I'm sure he will," Ponsonby said. "The traffic crawls. The bike would be faster, if anything."

Mary frowned. "Have we made it too obvious?"

"If she's not wearing it tomorrow," Ponsonby said. "We'll know we did, and she's found someone at the embassy to give it to."

Mary nodded. "The embassy staff would know better than to take a gift given to the princess, surely."

Ponsonby looked thoughtful.

"What is it?" Mary asked.

"It can't be a handover," he said. "It doesn't make sense."

"It may be that the embassy people know who she is but not all her secrets," Mary said. "For example, what if she'd been persuaded to join revolutionaries in Switzerland and something is in the brooch that advances their cause?"

Ponsonby considered this for a moment before saying, "There are a lot of weaknesses in that theory, but I take your point. We don't know what reason she has for behaving this way. We just have to be sure she can't hand over that brooch until it has been thoroughly examined."

"DCS Griffiths may be able to have the embassy burgled," Mary said. "I suspect he won't though, and nor would our secret service people. Too risky. The foreign office would be most upset if they lost a future friend, particularly one so handily placed in the region where most of the world's oil comes from."

"Then we must do it," Ponsonby said.

Mary shook her head. "We can't burgle the embassy either.

We have to track down that brooch and examine it or, better yet, have a copy made and exchange it so we have time to examine it at leisure. Its secrets may not be immediately obvious."

"If we prevent it being handed over," Ponsonby said as they reentered the house, "she'll have to keep it on her at all times until it can be handed over."

"Tomorrow, if she's wearing it," Mary said, "and if you're right, she will be, we steal and photograph it from every angle. I'll try to match the colors as well. I'm sure there's a jeweler in town who could make one quickly. The secret service will probably have one they use. I'll ask the chief superintendent."

DCS Griffiths was as difficult to convince as Mary thought he would be when she telephoned him.

"Lady Mary," he said, "young women, I'm sure, trade their jewelry the way boys trade cigarette cards. Why shouldn't this one do the same? It isn't really a diplomatic gift, and the old man wouldn't have given it to her if he believed it had some significance. It was probably just something valuable from his wife's jewelry box that he thought a young woman would appreciate."

"It's possible," Mary agreed, "and I thought of that too. An old man may not understand how quickly fashions in jewelry change, but it's the princess trying to give me the brooch that has made me suspicious."

"Surely, that's exactly why it's not suspicious," he said. "After all, she could have just left it in her jewelry box and never worn it again. Her bringing it to our attention could be an indicator that it's harmless. If she's playing some deep game, then it may even be a decoy, something to distract our attention from whatever else she's doing."

"I thought of that too," Mary said unhappily, "but it could mean there is something going on. I just can't discern what at this time."

"I'll advise the political powers that be," Griffiths said. "They won't like it. They will perceive us as amateurs playing in their game, playing badly at best and just plain stupid at worst."

"We can only make them aware," Mary said. "I'll have the Palace secretary pass on the warning too. They may have more weight in this than we have. After all, this is a royalty-to-royalty diplomatic venture."

Griffiths chuckled. "I'm sure they'll have more clout than I do."

"Do the police have any jewelers they use?" Mary asked.

"Not to my knowledge," Griffiths said. "The secret folks might. Why?"

Mary explained her exchange idea.

"I see," he said. "I can ask the shadowy figure who I liaise with on these occasions. I suggest you ask the Palace that question too or that 'gardener' you tell me is distracting the girls from their lessons."

"I will, and I'll secure that brooch somehow, even if I have to kill to retrieve it," she said with a wink of her eye.

"I will take that to mean you are very determined, Lady Mary," Griffiths said, laughing. "As a police officer, I can't hear things like that, and you should be more careful. This may yet turn out to be a dangerous game we're playing, and if anything should happen to the princess, words like those could come back to haunt you."

"You're quite right to warn me," Mary said, smiling, "for it is I who believes there is a dangerous game afoot and the police who suspect it's all just a coincidence."

"We aren't dismissing anything you say, Lady Mary, merely being cautious."

"Did your constable, the one that followed the princess home, witness anything suspicious?" Mary asked.

Griffiths laughed again. "No, but then our MI5 man was in the car, so the connection likely wouldn't approach the car. The princess would have to leave the car to make a secret handover, and that she didn't do."

THE WEATHER FORECAST said the following afternoon was to be warm, for May, which gave Mary the opportunity she was waiting for. She telephoned her assistants and had them ring the other pupils to instruct the debs that evening gowns were to be worn.

As she'd hoped, everyone obeyed. Wearing evening gowns was always popular in her day, and it proved to be so for this new generation. When she saw Jezebel hand her short spring jacket to the waiting Cook, she signaled Ponsonby to be ready. There was no need. His observant eyes had also caught the brooch leaving its momentarily distracted owner.

Lady Mary instantly set the students on an exercise that kept them mingling and talking, as if at a formal event. So long as she was kept busy, Jezebel might forget the brooch. Before the debutantes could grow tired of this exercise, Mary brought them together and set them to a new task.

Outside the ballroom, Cook handed over the jacket to Ponsonby, who whisked it down to the wine cellar where he'd set up his camera and equipment. The whole operation was over in minutes, and the jacket was hanging innocently on the coat rack long before Jezebel could have possibly remembered the brooch.

Mary observed Jezebel abandon the third exercise she'd set for the debutantes and suddenly dash out of the room. She returned moments later, smiling broadly, with the brooch now clipped to her gown's daringly low-cut bodice. Mary knew now she was right. That brooch meant something, and she, Mary, was going to discover what that was before too many days had passed, provided the princess's handlers and the MI5 agent, who would once again travel home with Jezebel, stopped her parting with it.

16

JEZEBEL IS THE PRINCESS

"Well?" Mary asked as the last of her students had left and Ponsonby emerged from the cellar door with two wet photos held by the corners.

"They're not dry yet," Ponsonby said, "but I was sure you'd want to look at them immediately."

"I do." Mary studied the photos as Ponsonby held them up to the light. "These are black and white. How will we match the colors?"

"Black and white was the film I had," Ponsonby said, "and the film I'm most familiar with using. It was too risky to try color film for the first time when we had so little time. Instead, I had Cook find me pieces of cloth and paper in the colors I remembered. She matched them as I set up the camera and took the pictures."

"Show me," Mary said.

"Cook has them safe, milady. I'll have her bring them to you."

With the photos laid on dinner plates and the color swatches nearby, Mary examined them carefully before nodding. "Yes.

This will do nicely. Thank you, Cook. Your assistance has been invaluable."

"Men can't match colors for toffee," Cook said, smiling mischievously at Ponsonby.

"It's true," Mary said. "I would ask Roland to bring my green shawl, and he'd bring a blue one. Hopeless."

"Like the duke, I'm also a little red-green color blind," Ponsonby said primly. "We never found it to be a handicap in anything significant."

Mary laughed. "It depends on your definition of significant." When Cook had left the room, Mary said, "Now, we need a jeweler to make this up by tomorrow. I wonder if that's possible?"

"We need Chief Superintendent Griffiths or one of your friends to provide a name," Ponsonby said. "Time is of the essence."

"Take these up to my room," Mary said, "and guard the door. No one in or out. I'll telephone everyone I know who might be able to help."

Griffiths, when she spoke to him, hadn't any names to provide, though he was still hoping a call might come through. His secret service counterpart had promised to try. Mary's acquaintances were either out or had no suggestions to make. She made her way disconsolately upstairs to inform Ponsonby of how little progress was being made.

"Our good fortune in securing the brooch," Ponsonby said, "means we have the information at hand when a jeweler is found, milady. We've been lucky, and that must mean something."

"It means we're going to be crushed with disappointment when a jeweler can't be found," Mary said, unwilling to admit to a bright side while time was slipping away.

"We must provide a copy of the brooch's design to a cipher

clerk and a language expert," Ponsonby said. "The message may be on the brooch, and we just can't see it."

"I asked Griffiths to drop in this evening, and we'll give him a copy for the police and others," Mary said.

"It's still a possibility this brooch is meant to distract us," Ponsonby said. "We must remain vigilant for other possibilities."

Mary nodded. "We don't have many days left. Whatever it is the princess is hiding, we have less than a week to uncover it."

"It may turn out to be something innocent," Ponsonby said. "For instance, she may have a Swiss boyfriend who's a commoner, and they're planning to elope. The real concern here is your safety, and that may have nothing to do with the princess. We should focus on your safety and let international diplomacy go its own way."

"Amen to that," Mary said, smiling. "Only I'm sure this is all about Jezebel, and I can't for the life of me understand why."

* * * * * 🐾 * * * * *

THE FOLLOWING DAY, a new twist to their preparations began. Jezebel claimed she had to leave the lessons and meet someone. She would return in only a matter of minutes.

"Your security men aren't here right now," Mary said. "I can't let you leave on your own. Perhaps my butler or the MI5 man could escort you."

"No!" Jezebel said. "It is a private, personal matter, and I will not have men involved." She paused. "Well, maybe the MI5 man would be acceptable."

"Then, I will go with you," Mary said.

Jezebel's tone when adding this last suggestion alarmed Mary, but she couldn't decide if it was because the girl might want to seduce the young man or hand over the brooch to him.

"It really is impossible for you to be alone outside," Mary said. "You know that. Your father's instructions are very clear."

"In Switzerland, I often went into town with the others," Jezebel said hotly. "My father didn't object. I'm not a world-famous celebrity like Marilyn Monroe. No one knows I'm here in London. Why would I be in danger here?"

"People do know you're here," Mary said. "It's been on the news. Your country and ours are negotiating an alliance, and you're here to further that. There may be many who would prefer that alliance didn't happen, and harming you would ensure that."

"I'm a princess, and I'm not from your country," Jezebel cried. "Neither you, nor anyone else here, has the right to interfere with my movements or my wishes, and I wish to leave now."

Mary frowned. What Jezebel said was true. She, Mary, had no authority to prevent her leaving, but the brooch was on Jezebel's dress right in front of her eyes, and Mary wasn't letting that go anywhere unseen.

"I will grab my coat," Mary said. "Cook and I will accompany you for your own safety. We won't interfere or eavesdrop with who you meet."

She turned and, with Jezebel following, left the ballroom.

"Ponsonby," Mary said, seeing him strategically placed in the entrance hall, as he always was when the lessons were in session, "Princess Jezebel and I are going for a walk. Have Cook fetch my coat, please."

Before they reached the door, Jezebel changed her mind. She shook her head. "This is intolerable," she said. "I will not attend any more of these nonsensical classes, and I will inform the Palace exactly why I have made this decision." She turned abruptly and marched back to the ballroom.

Mary followed slowly, to be sure to catch up Ponsonby and Cook on the change in plan. They were impassive when she did so, being careful not to betray any criticism of the princess's whims.

The class finished, and the students filed out, most chattering happily with their friends. Jezebel and her two hangers-on cast furious glares at Mary, who smiled sweetly in return.

Mary telephoned the Palace secretary immediately and explained what had happened and her actions. If Jezebel kept to her word, this might become a diplomatic incident and one that could only end with her own dismissal. Princesses, visiting foreign ones anyhow, could not be thwarted by people, no matter how high they stood in the social rankings.

"We must do what we can to smooth these choppy waters," Eleanor said. "You did right, of course, but…"

"I understand," Mary said, then, on a moment of inspiration, asked, "You wouldn't know of a jeweler who works quickly on private commissions, do you?"

"I know someone who makes jewelry for superior persons," Eleanor said. Mary could hear the broad smile in the secretary's voice as Eleanor continued, "How quickly it might happen, I can't say. He's very, um, different. He might do it today or in ten years. You can never tell."

"Would he do it in a day if you asked?"

"He might. A good story might decide the time he takes."

"It's a story of intrigue, romance, and murder," Mary said.

"Intrigue and murder should do it," Eleanor said. "How do we tell it without giving away the people involved?"

"Come to Culpeper House this evening, and we'll plot it together."

"Good evening, Chief Superintendent," Mary began when Ponsonby had finally been able to get him on the phone. "I have a concern I'd like to share with you."

"Ponsonby said," Griffiths replied. He sounded unenthusiastic.

"I know I was wrong about the petty thief being the attempted assassin," Mary said, "but if I don't share these things with you and one of them is right, there may be a serious incident we didn't prevent. Another murder, even. You wouldn't want that on your conscience, would you?"

"I'm listening," Griffiths said.

Mary had the sense of teeth being ground but continued, "How much do you know about the MI5 man?"

"I've told you how much," Griffiths said. "Very little and most of what I know is probably untrue. That's how these people work."

"Then can we be sure he isn't the person Jezebel is to hand off the brooch to?"

Griffiths sighed. "We don't know she's trying to hand anything off. She has been given a gift she didn't like. She offered it to you. You turned it down and persuaded her she had to keep it. She has kept it but brings it each day in the hope you, who might have a fondness for it, will change your mind."

"You don't believe that, I'm sure, Chief Superintendent."

"I'm keeping an open mind," he said. "She's a young woman in a foreign land who is doing things that look odd to the local people. That's as ordinary as it comes and not a sign of international espionage, in my everyday, ordinary opinion."

"We've strayed from the topic," Mary said. "Can you discover anything about the MI5 man?"

"In a word, no. I can try, only they will have done their jobs very badly if I learn anything I shouldn't."

"Please do before he walks off with the brooch and the secrets it contains."

"Lady Mary," Griffiths said slowly, "what you're asking could end my career and make you some serious enemies. These are the kind of people we say, with good reason, that we're pleased they're on our side. You are planning to put us on the other side."

Mary explained about Jezebel's decision to accept the MI5 man as an escort and no other.

"I've heard half the young women in those classes would happily have him escort them anywhere," Griffiths said sarcastically.

"He told me he spent time abroad as a young man..." Mary began.

"What he said, you can confidently disbelieve," Griffiths said. "The most I will promise is to make discreet inquiries to sound out his loyalties. No more than that, and even that's risky. They've been as jumpy as cats since those Soviet spies were identified in their ranks."

"If they were honest men," Mary said, "they would welcome information of the kind I'm supplying."

"In the world you and I inhabit, we sift through mountains of detail to find atoms of evidence to arrive at what we hope will be the truth," Griffiths said. "In their world, they construct elaborate realities to ensure the truth can never be found. Honesty isn't a trait they're familiar with. Believe me."

Mary laughed. "Your cynicism is too extreme, Chief Superintendent. Still, I'm holding you to your promise to look into our young gardener's background and satisfy me that he isn't the contact Jezebel is looking for."

She replaced the phone, and walking back to the drawing room, she rehearsed in her mind the elaborate reality she had prepared to help Eleanor win over the artist.

"INTERNATIONAL JEWEL THIEF?" Eleanor said. "Are there such people? Outside of books, I mean?"

"We believe so," Mary said seriously.

The story she'd decided on was outlandish in principle, often seen in fiction but rarely heard of in fact, but that was its selling point. It was plausible and intriguing, whereas a simple switch wouldn't capture anyone's imagination.

"Wouldn't a jewel thief recognize it as a forgery right away?" Eleanor asked. "I imagine they must be experts in such matters."

"It will be dark, and we mean to disturb him in the act so he hasn't time to examine it closely," Mary said.

"And DCS Griffiths has approved this?"

"He agrees with me," Mary said, "that the only way to smoke out this thief and catch him before he kills any more women is to lure him into a trap. My priceless old heirloom will be the bait once we've spread the story of it being recognized for what it is after languishing at the bottom of my family's old dress-up box for decades."

"Mother told me how brave you were in the old days," Eleanor said. "I recognize now she wasn't exaggerating. You could be killed before the police move in to arrest him."

"We will have things in place to keep me safe, you can be sure," Mary said, smiling in what she hoped was a modest manner.

"I'll telephone my artistic friend tonight and, with luck, will have these photos and color swatches to him first thing tomorrow," Eleanor said.

"Impress upon him how serious and urgent it is," Mary said. "Lives have been lost, and more are at stake."

"It's just like a movie," Eleanor said. "It's rather exciting, isn't it? I understand now why you do it."

Mary laughed. "Detecting is just frustrating most of the time, but sometimes, a moment like this comes along and makes it all worthwhile."

"Then I'll hurry things along by going straight from here to my friend's house," Eleanor said, rising from her chair.

As Mary walked her to the door and the waiting car, she said, "Telephone me as soon as you can. If he can't or won't do it at once, I need to find someone else."

The call, when it came, was late in the evening. Mary was preparing for bed when she heard it ringing and Ponsonby answering it. His footsteps on the stairs told her it was important, and she pulled on a robe and headed out to greet him.

"I'm on my way," she said, practically running down the stairs.

"He'll have it done by tomorrow afternoon," Eleanor told her. "In fact, he's working on it now. Who knew he was such a romantic and would be fired up by a story of derring-do? I must remember this for future requests."

Mary thanked her, replaced the handset, and found Ponsonby waiting. His expression was as impassive as ever, but she knew he was bursting with curiosity to know if the plan was in motion.

"Tomorrow afternoon," Mary said. "I hope before class finishes."

"How will we distract the princess to part with the brooch?" Ponsonby asked.

"I have all night to work out a plan," Mary said.

Before she'd begun to have a serious plan developed, Mary received a telephone call from DCS Griffiths.

"Chief Superintendent," Mary said, "this is a pleasant surprise. Have you discovered something?"

"I've discovered why the MI5 man is assigned to this case and that the princess is the real princess," he replied.

"All that from delving into the man's background?"

"He was in Tzatzikistan ten years ago with his family before all our people were kicked out. He actually played with the young Jezebel," Griffiths said.

"And he's sure this young woman is his old play friend?"

"He says when they spoke recently, she remembered him," Griffiths said.

"And how are we sure he's on the right side in all this international intrigue?"

"Our people have been grooming him from university," Griffiths said. "There's been no opportunity for him to develop opposing thoughts. It would have been spotted."

"You'll forgive me if I'm not fully persuaded, Chief Superintendent," Mary said, "and if Jezebel is an imposter, and he's claimed she isn't, I'm even less persuaded."

"But we don't know she's anything other than who she says she is, who the Tzatzikistan Embassy says she is, and who this young man who was a playfellow says she is," Griffiths said. "I think you really have to give up on that theory. She is the *real* princess."

Mary sighed. It did seem she'd been completely wrong thinking that somehow, despite all the evidence, Jezebel wasn't who she said she was. This final confirmation had to be the end of that line of inquiry.

"I see," she said after a moment. "Thank you, Chief Superintendent. I have to accept the evidence, and I will. Good night."

Disappointed, she placed the handset on its cradle. All the evidence pointed one way... except Dotty said the ankles were all wrong. Mary shook her head. Ridiculous. After all, who could believe a photo taken in a hurry at an event months before?

"You look troubled, milady," Ponsonby said as Mary passed him on her away from the telephone and back to her room.

"I am," Mary said. "I've just been told that the MI5 gardener is who he says he is, and he can confirm that Jezebel is who she says she is."

"That is good news," Ponsonby said. "It clears a lot of the fog that has surrounded our investigations."

"It should," Mary replied still doubtfully, "but I find I'd convinced myself she was an imposter and he was her contact, and I can't quite rid my mind of that impression."

"We all cling to our own ideas, even when evidence placed before us tells us we're wrong."

"I know, I know, but it is the only thing that makes sense," Mary said in an unhappy tone.

"Griffiths is sure of his information, I presume?"

"He says his informant is always reliable. I fear I've been on the wrong end of this from the start," Mary said.

"As we've no reason to disbelieve this new evidence," Ponsonby said, "I think we should look at everything again."

"I can't forget what Dotty said about Jezebel's ankles. The Jezebel in the photo was that bit bigger than the one we see, not just her ankles."

"Milady, young women of that age are very conscious of their size, their weight," Ponsonby said. "She saw her photos in the newspapers and slimmed, that's all."

Mary nodded. "I know, but Dotty is right. Not her ankles."

"The weight of evidence is against Dotty's observation," Ponsonby said. "We must focus on what is happening with the firm view that Jezebel is the princess and our MI5 man is not the contact. We must, milady. If we don't follow the evidence, we'll be lost."

"You're right, of course," Mary replied. "I'm just struggling to let go of a theory I thought I was calmly considering without any attachment but now find I was wedded to. Maybe I'm too old and set in my ways for the nimbleness of mind required to successfully solve riddles."

"I'm sure that isn't the case," Ponsonby said, "but maybe we're a little rusty."

Mary nodded. "But if Jezebel is the princess, why were Lady Hilary and Mrs. Bamford killed?"

"Perhaps there's someone else they would have recognized as being an imposter," Ponsonby said.

Mary groaned. "I hope not. Anyway, it can't be one of the girls, and there is no one else."

"Very true, milady," Ponsonby said, "and yet there must be a reason."

"We don't have much time left," Mary said. "Our only hope now is that the brooch is important in some way and DCS Griffiths is wrong about it being a decoy."

"I fear he may be right," Ponsonby said. "If the MI5 man isn't the contact, and we're assured he isn't, then the brooch isn't the important thing. Maybe tomorrow will bring a new clue."

17

BAIT AND SWITCH

"She's wearing the brooch," Ponsonby said quietly to Mary after he'd escorted the last of the students to the ballroom.

Mary had stayed away from their arrival so as not to upset Jezebel, in case she was still angry about Mary's refusal to let her leave alone on the previous day. The class was ready.

"And on her dress?" Mary asked. "Not on her jacket?"

"Precisely, milady," Ponsonby said. "She won't make that mistake again."

"I'm beginning to think you may be right, Ponsonby," Mary said. "The handover must happen here at Culpeper House—but to whom?" She sighed. "Well, we can do nothing until the replica arrives. Let me know the moment that happens."

She entered the ballroom to begin the lesson.

The previous evening, Mary had wrestled over many stratagems for stealing the brooch off Jezebel's dress or, in the wilder moments of the night, the dress off Jezebel. The young MI5 gardener figured a little too prominently in those scenarios for Mary's daytime comfort. In the end, she settled on an "accident" involving spilled drinks and generous cloths to mop up.

The cloth would "accidentally" pull the brooch off and

conceal the replica to be handed back with profuse apologies. It wasn't a great plan, but it was hard to find anything else at all. If only she, or Ponsonby, had trained as pickpockets or knew one locally, then something more subtle could have been devised.

The midday refreshments were served, in a way that mimicked the service at the ball, and Mary looked for Ponsonby to step in and give her the signal the brooch had arrived. This was the moment they thought the switch might be made. A clumsy maid or an excited assistant could jostle Jezebel's arm, and they would have their moment. However, Ponsonby didn't appear, and the refreshments were carried away without the switch being made.

Mary had arranged a second "refreshment" to happen later, if this moment was passed, as it had been.

"The dance masters are here," Mary told them, "and the next hour will be once again spent increasing your proficiency on the dance floor. It may be you will find yourself at the ball being invited to dance by a young man who is not a good dancer. This is an important occasion for you and for them. It will be best for all concerned that you make up for any shortfalls on their side, as I'm sure they will be happy to do for you. They are, after all, gentlemen."

As the music began and couples began to take the floor, Mary saw Ponsonby at the door. Keeping an eye on the room, she made her way to speak to him.

"We have the replica, milady," he said.

"Does it look and feel convincing?" Mary asked, though she was sure it would.

"It does, and I'm assured it weighs the same."

"Cook isn't too nervous?"

Ponsonby allowed himself a twitch of the lips before saying, "She is positively itching to give that young madam her come-uppance."

Mary smiled. "I wish we could include that other young madam, Chevallier, for Cook's sake, but we must be content with this one today."

Mary returned to the ballroom. The girls, dancing with bored expressions, were tired of the training. Now that she had the replica brooch, she would cancel all but one more class. Today was the day to make the switch.

Finally, it was time, the point where she'd provided the students with this additional refreshment break.

She clapped her hands. "Ladies!" She waited until they'd stopped and were regarding her with bored eyes. "We'll take our break and return to deportment after."

The young women groaned before breaking into their usual groups to talk while the refreshments were brought in.

Cook and Ponsonby carried trays into the room and placed them on the tables at the back of the room. Cook looked across the room at Mary, who nodded. Cook smiled and picked up a smaller tray and began placing drinks on it. Ponsonby, too, loaded a tray with small snacks, and the two began to circulate, serving the students who were too busily chattering about their lives to notice the servers.

As Cook moved ever closer to the princess, Mary stifled a smile and stiffened with the anticipation of the coming incident. She saw Jezebel holding forth, waving her arms as she usually did. The plan depended on that. Slowly, with Barkley at her heels, Mary made her way across the floor. She and Cook needed to meet at Jezebel's side at the same time. The moment arrived so quickly Mary was almost startled how easy it was.

Cook was at Jezebel's side but slightly behind when Mary said, "Jezebel, a word."

The princess turned, and her flailing arm hit the tray. Cook deftly sent the glasses and their contents forward onto Jezebel's dress. The tray clanged on the floor and glass shattered. Barkley jumped before stretching up to grab at Jezebel's long-sleeved glove.

"You stupid…" Jezebel stopped herself as she saw Mary's horrified expression. She began brushing her clothes with her hands and then swatting at Barkley, who was enjoying his moment of revenge at her past dismissals of him.

"Cook," Mary said. "Get cloths."

Cook hurried away, and Mary pounced. She ordered Barkley away as she removed her own silk shawl.

"Here, Princess," she said, "Let me help."

She mopped at the princess's bodice with her shawl, tangling it into the brooch. The brooch slipped off the bodice with the shawl, as it and the shawl fell toward the floor. Mary swiftly scooped both with her right hand. Clasping everything into the cloth, she carefully exchanged the real brooch for the imitation.

"I'm so sorry, Princess," Mary said, handing the fake to Jezebel. "Your brooch became tangled. Thankfully, it didn't fall and break."

Jezebel grabbed the brooch and gripped it firmly in her hand, her eyes blazing with fury. "Fire that woman immediately," she said, "and keep that dog away from me."

"It was my fault, not Cook's," Mary said. "I shouldn't have surprised you when she was so near with a tray of drinks."

"She threw it at me!" Jezebel shouted.

"She was just startled," Mary said. "Maybe, if you'll come with me, we can find something in my wardrobe for you to wear while your dress dries."

She gently drew Jezebel away by the arm, waving Cook, who was entering the room with a pile of towels, to stay out of Jezebel's line of sight. Cook took the hint and quickly retreated. She was nowhere to be seen when Mary and Jezebel stepped into the hall.

"Ponsonby," Mary said as she was guiding Jezebel to the stairs, "please tell the girls they may leave for the day, and I'll entertain them all again tomorrow at the same time, and call for the Princess's car, as well."

Fortunately, Mary still had some clothes from her slimmer days that the princess announced weren't too ugly for her to wear, though she was almost too furious to care. By the time Jezebel was tidy, Ponsonby announced her car had arrived, and she left with the curtest of farewells.

"Were you successful?" Ponsonby asked as the black car glided smoothly out into the street.

Mary took the brooch from the pocket of her frock and showed him.

"Now maybe we can identify what the fuss has all been about," Ponsonby said, smiling.

"I'm not sure two dead women can be considered fuss," Mary said seriously, "but I take your point."

Ponsonby nodded solemnly. "My words were ill-chosen. Excitement got the better of me."

Mary examined the brooch carefully. There was no obvious way of opening it. Did that mean the design on the scarab's carapace was the message?

"We need something sharp to open the back, milady," Ponsonby said.

"I'm not sure it does open," Mary said, handing it to him. "What do you think?"

Ponsonby examined the brooch and said, "I have a magnifying glass that may help."

He handed it back to Mary and left for his butler's pantry, where a host of unusual items were kept—unusual for a regular butler's pantry, though not for a butler who dabbled in crime detection.

When he returned, Mary had settled herself in the drawing

room, where light streamed in through the west-facing windows. She was examining the brooch from every possible angle.

"It must be a secret catch," she said as Ponsonby handed her the magnifying glass. "It's amazingly well made. I can't see a join anywhere."

"Then perhaps it's not in the body but on the head or legs," Ponsonby said.

"The legs aren't big enough for anything to be inside them," Mary replied. "I'm not sure the head is either."

She slowly turned the brooch under the magnifier and was about to give up in disgust when she saw what looked like a hinge. It was artfully included in a golden ornamental fringe across the creature's throat. If it was the hinge, the catch was at its tail. She turned the scarab quickly and examined the tiny detailed workmanship there.

Again, it took a moment before she saw what she had expected to find. Barely more than a whisker, the catch was hidden within the decoration. Searching in her nearby bag, she found her tweezers and pressed the catch. The underside of the body flopped open, and a small, single square of what looked like celluloid dropped out and landed on her lap.

Mary picked it up gently with the tweezers and said, "It's a photo negative, the smallest I've ever seen. Can your equipment blow it up enough to be legible?"

"Yes," Ponsonby said, "but we need this to go to the chief superintendent as soon as possible."

"And it will," Mary replied, smiling, "immediately after you have a copy of the photo for us to study."

Ponsonby took a silver tray from a nearby table and wiped it clean with a cloth. Mary dropped the negative on the tray, and Ponsonby placed the cloth over it. He walked as quickly as a butler was allowed to walk until he was out of Mary's sight, when he ran down the stairs to his dark room.

18

JUST NAMES

"I wish I'd studied Arabic lettering," Mary said, staring disconsolately at the photo Ponsonby had just delivered into her eager grasp.

"I'm afraid I, too, have no insight into anything here," Ponsonby said, "except to say it's a list of names."

"Or places," Mary said. "It's certainly a list."

"We must hope the police or secret service have translators they use," Ponsonby said.

"I'm sure they do, but until DCS Griffiths arrives and we can hand it over, we can never find out."

"Unfortunately, the one person we could ask is the person we stole it from," Ponsonby said. "Doesn't Your Grace have any acquaintances who have spent time in the Middle East?"

Mary shook her head. "I can't think of anyone. Our friends were all in India, Africa, Hong Kong, or the Caribbean. I don't think anyone was in Egypt, Iraq, or any of those places."

The doorbell rang, and Mary and Ponsonby exchanged glances.

"That will be DCS Griffiths," Mary said. "We should place

this photograph out of sight for now. He and his people can make their own from the negative."

"You suspect the police may have an informant among them?" Ponsonby asked, taking the photo from her.

"I don't know," Mary said. "Whoever killed our two ladies knew who to target. We should keep our own council until we know more."

Ponsonby left the room with the photo on a tray, which he placed carefully out of sight behind a stone figurine. Quickly, he crossed the hall and let Griffiths into the house.

"Good evening, Chief Superintendent," Ponsonby said as the footman took the policeman's coat and hat. "Lady Mary is expecting you. Follow me, please." He led Griffiths into the drawing room and announced him.

When the door was shut, Mary said, "We have something you need to see." She handed him a small envelope containing the negative.

"What is this?" Griffiths asked, carefully touching only the negative's edge with his finger.

"It's a negative," Mary said, keeping a straight face.

"I see that, but what of?"

"We hope your photo laboratory will tell us that," Mary replied.

"Where did you find it?"

Mary explained about the brooch, showing him the catch and door that had concealed the negative.

"This is stolen property," Griffiths said seriously.

"We can return it the way we got it," Mary said. "It's borrowed, not stolen."

"Hmm. I'm not sure the law would appreciate the subtle distinction," Griffiths said, grinning. "I assume Ponsonby has taken a print from this?"

Mary decided honesty was sometimes the best policy and agreed he had.

"And you can't discover anything from it?"

"Sadly, Arabic lettering isn't one of our skills," Mary said. "Even if it was, it will likely be in code."

"How long before this is missed, do you think?" Griffiths asked.

"I don't know," Mary admitted. "It depends if the princess is in on it or just an innocent courier."

"I thought we'd put the 'imposter' idea to bed? Never mind. What's your guess?"

"Innocent courier," Mary said, "for two reasons. One, even if she was an imposter, it's likely she was chosen solely on her appearance, which means she was unlikely to be part of whatever it is. Two, if, as you say, she's not an imposter, I can't comprehend those passing the message wanting a princess involved in whatever it is. She doesn't have the training for it."

Griffiths nodded. "May I have a copy of your print? I could get some of our Arabic contacts working on it before our lab has a print made. Every hour may count."

Mary looked quizzically at Ponsonby, who'd taken no part in the conversation until now.

"I took the liberty of making more than one print, milady," he said. "I'll give it to the chief superintendent as he leaves."

"Which is now," Griffiths said, rising from his chair. "The sooner we know what this is about, the better."

When Griffiths was gone, clutching the photo and the negative, Mary said to Ponsonby, "I'm glad you anticipated the need to provide Griffiths with a copy. Initially, I was leaning toward not giving him one."

"It's usually best in these matters to keep on the good side of the police, milady."

Mary nodded. "Usually, it is. What can we do to reward Cook for her part in the exchange?"

"My approbation should suffice, milady," Ponsonby said loftily. "That *should* be the way of things..." He paused and added, "But I suspect your commendation will be much appreciated."

"Then let her know I need to see her," Mary said, smiling at this insight into the ancient, lingering rivalry between senior staff at a great house. "Now, who do we know that understands Arabic writing?"

"I looked in Who's Who earlier," Ponsonby said. "There's a professor of Arabic Studies at Oxford, Clarence Aubrey, who I remember being a friend of the late duke during our time in the regiment. He might welcome an out-of-the-ordinary puzzle. Would you consider speaking to him, if I could find his telephone number?"

"Yes," Mary said. "Find him at once. If necessary, we'll motor down there tonight and deliver it into his hands."

"Very well, milady," Ponsonby said, leaving to begin the search.

PROFESSOR AUBREY WELCOMED them to his Oxford home and, when he had provided them both with a fine sherry, set to work translating the list they had provided.

"As you guessed," Aubrey said, looking up after only a moment of perusal, "it's a list of names."

"Do you recognize any of them?" Mary asked eagerly.

He shook his head. "I'm afraid not. They certainly aren't famous people. They're simply ordinary names. They could be from a telephone book. They're that sort of list."

"That's disappointing," Mary said. "I hoped we'd have the answer in this list."

"We may yet, milady," Ponsonby said. "If this is a list, then it must have a common source—important people in a company, for example or a list of members of an organization, perhaps."

Mary nodded. "But finding which company or organization the list refers to and why they are listed here will be difficult."

"I have many friends among the Middle Eastern community here in London," Aubrey said. "I'm sure it won't take more than one or two telephone calls to find what the list refers to."

"Then, Professor," Mary said, "please quickly finish your translation and make those calls."

Aubrey laughed. "The translation won't take much time. However, I would ask you to consider how I approach my friends. They may recognize the list for what it is. They may act on what I tell them in ways we wouldn't wish for."

"That's true, milady," Ponsonby said gravely. "We must be careful. These people's lives may already be in danger, or why this secrecy?"

Mary nodded. "I fear you're both right. This will need to be carefully handled." She fell silent as she considered how they might proceed without causing any more murders.

"How did you come by this list?" Aubrey asked.

"It was found in a place that leads us to believe it may be part of a plot," Mary said.

"So these may be plotters or loyalists," Aubrey suggested, "but which? And by whom?"

"That we don't know," Mary said thoughtfully. "And that makes it difficult to know how we might go forward."

"Well," Aubrey said, handing her a sheet of paper, "here is your list of names. You must now decide what to do with it."

"Thank you," Mary said, reading it quickly. "I'd like to sleep on this. May I telephone tomorrow for your further assistance?"

"Certainly," the professor said, "though I reserve the right to only assist if I can support what you propose."

"Of course," Mary said, preparing to leave. "Believe me, I, too, want to be sure we aren't putting lives in danger, and yet this list suggests maybe one side in a conflict has designs on the other, and that means someone will be hurt whatever we do."

"We Westerners interfere too much in other people's affairs, in my opinion," said Aubrey. "Nevertheless, I will do what I can."

He escorted them out and lingered in the doorway as Ponsonby drove the car out of the drive and onto the road back to London.

"The professor is very close to the Arab community in London, milady," Ponsonby said as he saw the professor disappear from the rearview mirror. "We may have made a mistake there."

Mary nodded. "It seems incredible that he knew none of the names on the list. It's a long list. Can we even be sure he translated them correctly?"

"Quite," Ponsonby said, catching her eye in the mirror. "We won't know that for sure until we get a hold of the police list."

"And that might be too late," Mary said bitterly. "I hate these spy games they play. Nothing, and no one, is trustworthy. I'll telephone the chief superintendent and ask him to hurry his people."

"He won't be pleased that we've brought others into the investigation," Ponsonby said.

"He would hardly have an investigation if it wasn't for us," Mary said, "so he can be as angry as he likes. It won't upset me one bit."

Ponsonby smiled faintly, which was as close to a laugh as he was prepared to go.

Ponsonby was right. Mary telephoned the moment she was

in the house, and Griffiths was angry that the people on the list had been made known to a member of the public.

"You should have waited for our people to translate," Griffiths said.

"Professor Aubrey is a serious scholar and highly respectable," Mary replied sharply, "and if anything happens to members of the London Middle Eastern community in the next few days, we'll know who to go to for answers. The professor must realize that."

"That will be no comfort to the victims," Griffiths reminded her. "We have two people already dead in this strange affair. I doubt the killers will spare the professor if he alerts them."

"Regular crime seems so much cleaner," Mary said unhappily. "This underhand, treacherous world of espionage disgusts me."

"Then maybe you should leave it to the experts," Griffiths said.

"I think not," Mary retorted. "My predecessor in the job was killed, and a nice woman who only wanted to renew an old acquaintance was murdered too. That's too close for comfort. I'm not waiting for the wheels of officialdom to grind out an answer."

Griffiths laughed. "Your faith in us isn't encouraging, Your Grace."

"I know you'll sort it out, Chief Superintendent," Mary said, relaxing a little. "I just have a more pressing schedule than you do. The ball is days away, and I want to be there."

"I'll have our translators working on it the moment they arrive. I should have a list to compare with yours very early tomorrow morning."

"Thank you," Mary said. "Perhaps bring your list here so we can compare the spellings. Our pronunciations over the telephone may not match, and we could waste time on simple errors."

THE LISTS, when compared, were as identical as could be expected of people translating foreign names into English.

"That's a relief," Ponsonby said as they finished the comparison. "At least we know the professor dealt honestly with the translation."

"We don't know he won't be as honest about keeping the list to himself," Mary said.

"We don't," Griffiths said, "but I take Mr. Ponsonby's earlier point. He should have recognized many of these people. They're most of the Tzatzikistan Embassy staff."

"That may not mean anything," Mary said. "After all, a professor at an out-of-town university doesn't necessarily meet with embassy staff in the capital."

"I'm sure you're right, milady," Ponsonby said. "I'm just nervous because I will feel responsible if anything should happen."

"It leaves us with a puzzle, though," Mary said. "If many of the names are of respectable names of embassy staff, and the others may also be equally innocent, why is this list important?"

"Perhaps they aren't innocent," Griffiths said. "Maybe they're plotting something, and this list tells the king so he can arrest them."

"It's just a list of names," Mary said. "They'd just shrug it off. There would have to be proof of their treachery for it to mean anything."

"Was there nothing else inside the brooch?" Griffiths asked.

"Nothing," Mary and Ponsonby said together.

"Then there must be a second package," Griffiths said.

Mary shook her head. "The list and the proof must go together. One without the other would be worthless." She frowned. "Can your translator come here quickly?" she asked Griffiths.

"The design," Ponsonby said. "It has to be the design."

Griffiths practically ran to the telephone. A minute's argument with the translator's department head ended with the most knowledgeable of them on his way to Culpeper House.

"I wish now we'd asked the professor's opinion on the design too," Mary said to Ponsonby while Griffiths was hanging up the telephone with a final thump.

"If the translator isn't knowledgeable about Arabic decorative art, we may have to," Ponsonby replied.

As Ponsonby had feared, the translator was knowledgeable about words, but the design on the scarab's back meant nothing to him.

"Sorry I couldn't be of more help, sir," the man said as Griffiths thanked him for his time.

"Not your fault," Griffiths said, smiling. "It was just possible the design was stylized words, but we need an art expert."

When the man was gone, Griffiths said, "I suggest we ask your professor if art is his forte, and if it isn't, we head for the London School of Middle Eastern Studies right away."

"Maybe we should go there first," Mary said. "It will be quicker than a drive to Oxford, and I'm still not comfortable that Professor Aubrey claimed not to know any of the names on the list."

"Suspicion is a terrible thing," Griffiths agreed. "However, I'll find out who is our contact at the school, and we'll be on our way."

It was almost lunch time before they left Culpeper House to meet with the Middle Eastern Art expert the police used and, thanks to London traffic, well past the arranged time when they arrived.

Professor Standish was a younger man, surprisingly so for such an eminent expert.

"I grew up in the Middle East," he explained when Mary commented on his youth. "My father worked throughout the region all through my childhood, and I was fascinated by everything I saw. Naturally, I studied the subject at university. My years out there weren't wasted, you see."

He smiled as he led them into his office. There, he examined the brooch by eye and then with a magnifying glass, nodding seriously as he did so.

"Well?" Griffiths demanded when the silence had grown too much to bear.

"I'm fairly sure the design is a small piece from a larger picture," Standish said. "I need to consult to be sure, but if I'm right, it refers to a moment in history and concerns the betrayal of a king."

"How long do you need to consult?" Mary said, though she had no doubt his guess was correct.

"The books I need are in the school's library," Standish said. "An hour or two should be sufficient. May I take the brooch?"

"It will be best if we all come with the brooch, Professor," Griffiths said, grinning as he saw Lady Mary's expression. "It's not ours to lose, you see."

"I'm not in the habit of stealing things," Standish said stiffly.

"I've no doubt of it," Griffiths said affably, "but it's valuable, it's evidence, and it isn't ours. We will all go to the library."

Standish was correct in his estimate. Within the hour, he was able to show them a photo of an ornate design from a wall hanging, vivid red and gold threads snaking their way through the fantastical Palaces and gardens of what was presumably a royal

Palace. The design on the brooch was just one small detail that appeared almost at the end of the tale.

"It tells of the treachery by the king's supposed friends and relatives," Standish said. "An odd choice of subject for a brooch."

"Perhaps," Mary said quickly, "the brooch was given as a warning of a false lover or something of that kind." She didn't want a second professor alerting his contacts in the Middle Eastern community.

Standish nodded. "Yes," he said, "that might be it. If the recipient of the brooch was a scholar, the meaning would be plain enough."

"Professor," Mary said as they prepared to leave, "you said you lived in the Middle East as a child. Were there many other young Englishmen there? That you knew of?"

He shook his head. "Not too many. Most parents left their sons in boarding schools here in England. We saw some occasionally during the holidays. Why do you ask?"

"Oh, we have a young gardener who says he, too, followed his father abroad during his childhood. Like you, I thought children were generally in schools at home, and it intrigued me that I should meet two exceptions to the rule so quickly."

"I'm sure the demands of the empire meant there were others like me and your gardener," Standish said. "A minority, perhaps, but not unusual, I expect."

"I expect you're right," Mary said.

"What is his name?"

"I'm afraid I only know him as John," Mary said, smiling. "If I'd known of your background, I would have come prepared."

"Is it important?"

"I don't think so," Mary replied. "The thought just came to me." She bid him good day.

The drive back to Culpeper House was almost in silence, for now the group wasn't even sure if the police driver was safe.

Only when they were alone in the drawing room could they find it possible to speak openly.

"It seems the people on the list are traitors," Ponsonby said as he was serving sherry and taking one himself at Lady Mary's insistence.

"And from our government's point of view," Griffiths said, "which group are the desirable ones for our government to promote? It wouldn't do for us to expose the plot, only to find our government is behind it."

"This is why I dislike espionage so much," Mary said. "Who can we ask without giving the game away?"

"I have to report to my superiors, and they will report to the Special Branch and the secret service," Griffiths said. "My only option is *when* I report."

"Normally," Mary said, "I'd say report and let the chips fall as they may, but I'd hate for poor innocent folks to get caught up in the wrong place at the wrong time."

The three lapsed into thoughtful silence, each brooding on the responsibility they were assuming by their actions, sipping their sherry while they coldly considered condemning people they didn't know.

"Is Jezebel the real princess, an active participant in the treachery, or just an innocent dupe who was hired for the part with no idea what she was getting herself in for?" Ponsonby asked. "If she's innocent, we need to protect her the moment we report this."

"I agree," Mary said. "I don't like her, but if she's a struggling actress hired for her likeness to the real princess, we must do what we can for her. Whatever has happened, to the real princess and others, she may not have been responsible for."

"Not that again," Griffiths cried. "We know she's the princess. The question is only has she been duped or is she in on this plot, whatever it is. And I can only hold off an hour or two. Otherwise, I'll be the scapegoat for everything that goes wrong."

"Could we invite her here?" Ponsonby asked. "Detain her and hold her somewhere until you've made your report?"

"That's kidnapping," Griffiths said. "I couldn't possibly agree to that."

"Could you hold her on some trumped-up charge?" Mary asked.

"No, I could not!" Griffiths was even more upset at this suggestion.

"Then we have to hope that, if she's working innocently, she'll be protected by her guards, and if she's one of the plotters, she'll be pulled out of the embassy by her friends before the king's men arrive to arrest her," Mary said.

"I'm afraid so," Griffiths said. "There can be no other way. We can't alert her or them, whoever they are."

Nodding, Mary asked, "Then what can we do in the short time before you hand all this over to your superiors, Chief Superintendent, that might show us which are the good people and which are the bad?"

"I've thought about it," Griffiths said. "There's no point in holding off. Nothing we learn will help us at all."

Mary looked at Ponsonby to observe if he had any suggestions. He shook his head.

"Then I suggest you drive straight back to the Yard with the evidence and begin the process," Mary said, "before we do something silly."

"You won't warn the princess?" Griffiths asked suspiciously, staring into the eyes of each to look for wavering.

"We won't," Mary said, "though it gives me a horrible sinking feeling in my stomach over what comes next."

"By the way, what was behind your question to Standish?" Griffiths asked. "The one about growing up abroad."

"As I explained to the professor," Mary said. "The coincidence of two such young men in this small series of events struck me as we talked."

"But Standish only came into this today and at our invitation," Griffiths replied.

"I know," Mary said. "It just struck me there was another route for possible intrigue I hadn't previously considered."

"I thought we'd decided our MI5 man can't be part of the plot," Griffiths said, "or the brooch would have been handed over days ago, and he would be long gone by now."

"Yes," Mary said slowly. "It's just my suspicious nature getting the better of me."

When Griffiths was gone, Mary and Ponsonby walked back to the drawing room.

"Whichever way this goes, milady," Ponsonby said, "one side or the other was going to come to a sticky end. We haven't led to lives being lost, milady. We just may have changed which lives will be lost."

"I know, but even that is of little comfort. Maybe we've sent the better of the two sides to their deaths."

"And maybe the worst side, milady. Let's not forget we can't know the future and who would have acted better than the other."

"Isn't that a Doris Day song?" Mary said. "Que sera sera?"

"I believe it is, milady," Ponsonby said somberly, "and most apt, if I may say so."

He exited the room, leaving Mary to stare into the flames of the fire burning on the hearth. It was May and normally past fires in the rooms, but the mornings and evenings were still cool. Cook, she thought, was rewarding her with some physical warmth for allowing her to have a part in Jezebel's downfall.

As she ate breakfast the following morning, Mary heard the telephone ring and Ponsonby making his way to answer it. She listened intently, holding her uneaten toast halfway to her mouth, for even the crunching of toast might make it hard for her to hear.

Ah, it was urgent. Ponsonby was on his way to tell her who it was, and he wouldn't do that unless he thought she'd want to know immediately.

"Who is it?" Mary asked as the butler entered the room.

"DCS Griffiths, milady. He wishes to let you know what has been decided."

Ponsonby was right. She did want to take this call.

Mary practically skipped from the table and across the floor to the telephone, her stomach in knots.

"Good morning, Your Grace," Griffiths said.

"Never mind that," Mary said. "What's happening?"

"The people who run these things in our spy agencies want everything to go on as before. They want to follow where the brooch goes and to who. They want to *roll up the whole gang*, is how they put it."

"You mean I'm supposed to have the princess here in my training class today as if nothing was happening?" Mary cried. "I'm not an actress. She'll see straight through my pretense."

"It won't matter," Griffiths said "We've pretended to remove the watchers, so she can do with the brooch whatever it is she's supposed to do with it. New, unfamiliar observers have taken their place."

"The sooner she gives it away," Mary said thoughtfully, "the better."

"Yes, that's the key to this business. She has to hand it over, but who to?"

"The man who gave the brooch to Jezebel presumably expected it to be passed along," Mary wondered. "Would her father likely have been the brooch's final destination?"

"Maybe, maybe not," Griffiths replied. "We still aren't certain if the list is of loyalists or traitors, so we need to let the exchange happen and witness who collects."

"Maybe my poor acting will be enough to start the chain in motion," Mary said.

"I'm sure you will do splendidly, Lady Mary," Griffiths said encouragingly.

Mary thanked him for his faith in her abilities and returned to her breakfast.

"Well, milady?" Ponsonby said as he returned to the breakfast room.

"Today's class is on," Mary said, "and we're to behave toward the princess as if we know nothing about brooches, lists, or international espionage plots."

"Very good, milady," Ponsonby said. "They hope to catch the exchange taking place?"

"They do. They want to catch all the plotters, whoever they may be."

"I hope the exchange won't be here," Ponsonby said. "I still feel there's a chance the go-between may be someone in Culpeper House. Why else would she wear it here?"

"Then it has to be the MI5 man, John, pretending he is our gardener," Mary retorted, "because it isn't you, me, or Cook, and they can't have known anyone else would be hired for the season, and if it is, everything we were told about him was wrong."

Ponsonby allowed himself a small twitch of the lips to show

his agreement before saying, "John isn't here today, milady. There's a new man, so it seems the handover is to someone else."

"I'm glad to hear it," Mary said. "Even when I was suspecting him, I couldn't help liking him." She shuddered and continued, "I do hope she hands it over, and the plotters, whoever they are, are all in jail by the end of the day. This has been most unpleasant."

The handover of the brooch hadn't taken place by the time Jezebel arrived at Culpeper House for the afternoon class. The brooch was still displayed on the light spring Dior jacket she was wearing.

Mary and Ponsonby spied on the young women through the partly open door of the ballroom before Mary was set to make her entrance.

"I can't help feeling you're right," Mary said, puzzled. "She always wears it here. Why? Does she know what it contains and she must never let it out of her sight, or is the exchange taking place here or on her journey here and back?"

"I think it must be on the journey, milady," Ponsonby said. "If you remember, one time she was here with it, she tried to leave early and without her guards."

Mary nodded. "And yet..." She paused. "Never mind. It's no longer our concern. It's in the hands of the police and the authorities. They must sort it out."

"Your students are becoming restless, milady," Ponsonby said, indicating the young women who were indeed beginning to question why they were here without their teacher in attendance.

Mary sighed. "Show in the dance and deportment masters when they arrive. I'll begin without them."

She entered the room and clapped her hands to grab the attention of her students while Ponsonby closed the door behind her.

19

REVELATIONS

After the students had left, Mary, Winnie, Margie, and Dotty remained in the drawing room waiting. They talked some, but for the most part, an anxious silence reigned. The grandfather clock in the hall chimed each quarter of an hour and then the hour until Ponsonby and Cook brought sandwiches at seven o'clock.

"This waiting is the worst," Mary said to Ponsonby as she nibbled on a sandwich.

"Starving yourself won't help, milady," Cook said in her usual blunt fashion.

Mary smiled. "That's very true. Sadly, knowing that doesn't unknot my insides."

"Mine either," Winnie agreed as she, too, struggled with a cucumber sandwich.

The others agreed, and silence again descended.

Before Cook gave up and started removing the food, the doorbell jangled clamorously. Ponsonby forgot he was a butler and shot out of the room like a rocket. A moment later, he entered with Griffiths in tow.

"Well?" Mary demanded too eager for news to be bothered with pleasantries.

"I'm on my way to the House of Commons," Griffiths said, "to brief the home secretary, but I thought as I was passing, you'd like to know what's happening.

"We would, Chief Superintendent," Mary said, "and as you're in a hurry, make it quick."

Culpeper House's large drawing room was the perfect place to catch the story, Mary thought, as her three proteges sat nervously on the sofa, with Ponsonby standing majestically aloof behind her and she enthroned in her favorite chair. Chief Superintendent Griffiths looked like a lecturer standing before them, preparing to tell his news.

"Please begin, Chief Superintendent," Mary said as he hesitated. "Tell us what the police have done with the information we provided you."

Griffiths grinned at this sally but didn't rise to the bait. "We are all aware of how much you have all contributed to what I'm about to tell you," he said.

"Well, I wish you would tell us," Mary said, exasperated. "The suspense is killing me. Did you arrest Jezebel? Is she a princess or not?"

Griffiths laughed. "If I can get a word in, I'll tell you."

Silence greeted this remark. He looked at each expectant face and, when he was sure there'd be no more interruptions, began. The moment he spoke, however, the telephone rang, and he stopped.

"That may be for me," he said.

"Ponsonby can find out while you start," Mary said, and Ponsonby again forgot he was a butler and ran to the telephone.

"We followed the car with Princess Jezebel in it, and as we'd all expected, it stopped no more than a mile from here. The princess stepped out and briefly spoke to a young man our security people recognized. The handover of the brooch was done so discreetly I'm sure anyone who might have witnessed it would never have known what happened. We, of course, could see it was no longer on the princess's lapel."

"So she really was the princess?" Winnie asked.

"I'm telling the events as they unfolded," Griffiths said. "At this point, the young woman was just Princess Jezebel."

"So she wasn't the princess?" Margie cried. "I knew it."

"Patience, please," Griffiths said. "To continue, there were now two trails. The first, following the princess and the other, following the brooch."

"And neither of them suspected they were being followed?" Dotty blurted out, unable to stop herself.

"They did not," Griffiths said, enjoying the excitement that his tale was generating in his audience. "Here's where the story becomes shocking."

He looked about and grinned. They were shifting in their seats and leaning forward with interest.

"Detective Chief Superintendent," Ponsonby said, reentering the room, "you're to leave immediately. The politicians are growing impatient."

Griffiths' expression said clearly what he thought of impatient politicians, but he nodded. "I'm sorry, everyone. It's more than my job's worth to keep these people waiting. I'll return, and when I do, I should have even more information."

His listeners groaned in disappointment as he hurriedly left the room, Ponsonby following behind him.

After reentering the drawing room, Ponsonby said, "The chief superintendent gave me a little more of the story as we walked to the door."

"Tell us!" the group practically shouted.

"The agent with the brooch traveled quickly across town to a house of a well-known Tzatzikistan citizen, a wealthy man whose loyalty to the king was considered to be certain. They assume he wanted the list to hand to the king to prove his faith." Ponsonby paused and tilted his body for dramatic effect, before saying, "The young woman, Jezebel, unfortunately disappeared."

A moment of silence passed.

Stunned, Mary said, "She couldn't just disappear. She was in a car being followed through London streets."

"I'm afraid that was all the chief superintendent was able to impart before he got into his car," Ponsonby said. "We have to wait."

"You girls may have to go home," Mary said in disgust. "It could be the middle of the night before we receive more information."

"I'll call my mother," Winnie said. "She'll let me stay."

"Me too," Margie said

"And me," Dotty added.

With the calls made, the group returned to the drawing room to wait. Occasionally, someone would suggest doing something to divert their minds, but no one had the heart for diversions. Each sat or wandered the room as their feelings moved them.

By nine o'clock, Cook and Ponsonby decided they all needed sustenance and announced they would go to the kitchen and make cocoa. They returned with cocoa and biscuits to ward off what they knew would become hunger pangs as the night wore on.

"Milady," Ponsonby said, seeing the younger sleuths yawning discreetly, "perhaps some of us could rest for a time and then come back to relieve the others?"

Mary nodded. "Good idea. Now, who will take the first watch with me?"

"I will," all three assistants said together.

Mary laughed. "We need to have someone to relieve us later."

Cook said, "I'll rest now and relieve you at two, if the Chief Superintendent hasn't returned with news by then."

"Thank you," Mary said. "What about you Ponsonby?"

"I don't sleep much nowadays," he said. "I'll stay with both you and Cook."

"Very well." Mary paused. She'd seen the slightest of glances pass between Cook and Ponsonby that momentarily startled her before she continued, "Now, girls, who will take the graveyard shift with Cook?"

After a brief discussion, Margie and Dotty agreed to rest and return later but only on the promise they would be awakened *the moment* DCS Griffiths returned.

With that assurance given, Mary, Ponsonby, and Winnie settled in with their needlework for what they hoped wouldn't be a long wait.

Midnight was chiming on the hall clock when they heard the doorbell jangle, its clamor even louder in the night's silence.

Ponsonby went to greet Griffiths and lead him to the drawing room before going to wake Cook and send her to rouse the girls.

Back in the drawing room, he found Mary had already invited Griffiths to pour himself a whisky, one for her, and a sherry for Winnie. Normally, his dignity as a butler would have been offended by such behavior, but he let it pass.

"The others will be here soon, milady," Ponsonby said.

They were. Their excitement wouldn't let them dawdle.

Ponsonby poured them, and himself, drinks and they were ready to learn the news.

Mary began, "You told Ponsonby that Jezebel, or whoever she is, disappeared from the car in a crowded street, but that couldn't be possible, could it?"

Griffiths rubbed his face where weariness had etched deep

lines on his brow. "No, but that's how it appeared to the man following her. The car entered a narrow street filled with shoppers and loiterers who swarmed around it, and at that point, our observer noticed the car was empty except for the driver."

"She must have jumped out into the crowd," Winnie suggested.

"Yet our man saw no one who looked like the princess among the mass of people, as he made his way through it."

"Maybe she changed in the car," Margie cried. "Many of us do that between engagements."

"No doubt," Griffiths said. "At present, we've got eyes on all ports and airports to ensure that she doesn't escape."

"So you know she wasn't the princess," Mary said.

"We do now," Griffiths said, "because about an hour after 'our' Jezebel disappeared, the real Jezebel turned up at the Tzatzikistan Embassy in Paris. She claims she was kidnapped in Switzerland on her way to the airport and has been held ever since. Her two guards were in on the plot, holding her in Switzerland at first and then transporting her to Paris. She was unconscious when being moved and kept in windowless rooms the rest of the time. She couldn't help us at all."

"They let her go when they got the list?" Margie asked.

"Yes, they did. We can only surmise the revolutionaries were doing their best not to set the world against them by killing a princess of the Tzatzikistan Royal Family."

"They had no hesitation killing two harmless women who were in their way, though," Mary said grimly.

Griffiths nodded. "Yes. We can't account for that yet, except maybe there was a change of leadership when someone realized that killing innocent bystanders was going to be a problem for them if they took power."

"Why did they kill them, though?" Dotty asked, puzzled.

"Because both of them knew the real Jezebel," Mary said. "I thought that must be it."

"Exactly right," Griffiths said. "Both women had seen the real Jezebel on more than one occasion, and they would become suspicious of the fake Jezebel, particularly if she couldn't recall incidents from her own past."

"But..." Mary began, then said, "Chief Superintendent, the actress wasn't in a traveling production of a Somerset Maughan play last autumn, was she?"

"I couldn't say, Lady Mary. Why?"

"It would explain why I was attacked," Mary said. "They thought I might recognize her. Have you caught her? Was she one of them or just a look-alike hired to play the part?"

"You've jumped ahead in the story, Lady Mary," Griffiths said. "We haven't rounded them all up yet, at least not in my recounting of the story."

"Is that why you took so long to come back, Chief Superintendent?" Ponsonby asked.

Griffiths nodded. "The principal leaders of the gang didn't arrive at the businessman's house until late evening. We're sure there are smaller fish out there, but we're confident we have the ringleaders."

"And are they talking?"

"They were offered deals to talk," Griffiths said. "It's the classic prisoner's game. If they all stay silent, they might be able to ride it out, only we said they'd be sent to Tzatzikistan unless they talked and that, naturally, whoever talks first goes free and the others are doomed. They all talked."

"The fake princess?" Margie asked.

"She's a young refugee from Tzatzikistan who has been doing acting work here. She was brought here by her parents who fled the country between the wars. Her resemblance to the real princess is remarkable."

"I would have thought an actress would have been better able to play the role," Winnie said. "She wasn't convincing."

"Maybe it's because she isn't a good actress. That has prevented her from winning many parts on the London stage," Griffiths said, smiling, "but maybe she was told the real princess was arrogant and dismissive of servants and others. I suspect she was doing her best to make this role seem right to anyone who'd heard the princess was that way."

"She must have known how dangerous this was," Mary said.

"If she didn't at first, I'm sure she did when she reported that Mrs. Bamford wanted to meet with her and then learned Mrs. Bamford had been murdered," Griffiths said. "We're interviewing her parents right now. Whether or not she's an actual revolutionary, I suspect she's at least a sympathizer. Her parents are pretty Bolshie anyway."

"Was it a Communist plot?" Ponsonby asked.

"More personal than communist, I'd say," Griffiths replied. "The ones we've arrested just hate King Raheem."

"She's still going to be in danger if her part in this is known to the government over there," Mary said. "She can't have realized what she was getting herself into."

Griffiths shrugged. "We haven't found her yet, so we don't know. If she can persuade our people she was innocent, she may be all right."

"And the people on the list?" Margie asked.

"What happens to the list is decided way above my lowly rank," Griffiths said. "Almost the whole London Embassy was on the side of the revolution, as well as many here in the local community. I imagine it will depend on whether our government thinks it can deal better with the revolutionaries or the king as to what happens to those on the list."

Mary shivered. "You mean if our people believe the king is

the better bet, the list goes to him and all those on that list will most likely be killed?"

"Yes," Griffiths said, "but the reverse is also true. If our people think the revolutionaries are the best option, the king, his family, government, and supporters would be killed. There's no saving of lives in either case."

"That's awful," cried Dotty, horrified.

"I'm afraid it's the way of life in the wider world," Mary said quietly. "There's no escaping it, much as we'd like to." She paused before turning to Griffiths and asking, "When might we know?"

"Soon, I imagine," Griffiths said. "This isn't a decision they can delay."

THE FOLLOWING DAY, BBC radio news informed the world a revolutionary coup against the Tzatzikistan government had been foiled in London and all the plotters arrested.

Mary and Ponsonby, listening together as they waited for the students to arrive for their final class, glanced at each other.

"I wish we had never become involved," Mary said.

"Milady, we must keep in mind that those people killed two innocent women," Ponsonby said. "Even if their cause was just, those deaths make them simply murderers."

Mary nodded. "Fortunately, there'll be no Jezebel at today's class, not the real or the fake. According to Griffiths, when he telephoned earlier, the real one's being kept in a secret place until all this is settled."

"It's in the plotters' favor," Ponsonby said, "that they released the true princess alive."

"Yes," Mary replied. "Different branches of the organization, possibly, one more moderate than the other. I doubt it will save them when they're returned to Tzatzikistan, however."

"I hear the first cars arriving," Ponsonby said. "I expect there'll be questions. They're sure to have heard the news."

"Fortunately, we know nothing," Mary said, "and we must hope our three assistants keep their heads and their silence too."

LATER THAT EVENING, the doorbell rang, jangling Mary's nerves afresh. She heard Ponsonby open the door and greet DCS Griffiths. A moment later, they entered the drawing room.

"Good evening, Chief Superintendent," Mary said, smiling warmly. "What brings you out at this late hour?"

"I thought you should know," he replied, taking the seat she offered, "we've caught the fake princess."

"At least she's alive," Mary said. "The lack of news about her was making me fear the worst."

"Quite understandable," Griffiths said, taking the glass of whisky Ponsonby handed to him. "You should know she will likely involve you in her defense if it comes to trial."

Mary shot upright. "What? Why?"

"It seems she offered to give you the brooch and you forced her to keep it. From the moment that Patricia Bamford was killed, she'd been terrified for her life. Until then, she thought it was no more than a game, a good cause. When she realized it wasn't and came to you for help, you turned her away."

"I simply told her she had to keep it for her father and his old friend's sake," Mary said. She couldn't believe any of this.

Griffiths grinned. "I don't think you should worry. There's no appetite for prosecuting her so far as I can tell."

"Then what will happen to her?" Ponsonby asked him. "She

wasn't a likable person, but if she really was misled into taking part, I can't feel anything bad should happen."

"If she talks and gives good information," Griffiths said, "I imagine the secret service will squirrel her away somewhere safe with a new name. If she's left on our doorstep, the police I mean, witness protection is a good hiding place."

"This all depends on her being a genuine innocent, I imagine," Mary said.

Griffiths nodded. "Time will tell on that."

"And our other mystery character, the gardener?"

"I can't help you there," Griffiths said. "He's vanished, as these people do when their job is finished."

"But someone must know who he is," Mary protested.

"I assure you *that* someone isn't me or anyone in the police force," Griffiths said, smiling. "They don't tell mere mortals what they do."

"He spoke of his father and family. Maybe we could find him that way," Mary wondered aloud.

"I suspect that was his cover story, Lady Mary," Griffiths said, shaking his head. "It's unlikely to be real. Why do you want to meet him again?"

"I would like to know that he really wasn't their contact," Mary said. "I don't want to learn he was one of them, and he may harbor a grudge against us for meddling."

Griffiths frowned. "My contact said he was no longer part of the operation. I took that to mean he was reassigned."

"That's ambiguous," Mary said. "I would prefer to hear something more positive, something more specific about him."

"They'll never say," Griffiths said.

"Ask your contact for assurance my life isn't at risk," Mary said. "They could at least give me *that*."

Griffiths nodded. "I'll try, but I must get home. I wanted you to know what I hope is the end of this sad business in case it isn't and you're suddenly called in as a witness."

Mary rose and followed him from the room. "I hope we shall keep in touch, now we've met again," she said as they walked to the door.

Griffiths stopped. He turned and said, "I'd like that too." He smiled and exited the door Ponsonby was holding open.

20

ONE DOOR CLOSES. A NEW ONE OPENS

Queen Charlotte's Ball was a grand affair, quite as glittering as Mary remembered it to be, and she beamed with pride that all her pupils acquitted themselves flawlessly. Even the unfortunate Louise Coalthorpe's cheeks were rosy and her smile bright, a significant improvement she had gained from the classes. Onerous as they'd seemed, the lessons had paid off, and nothing could rival the elegance of the debutantes.

Mary inconspicuously wiped at an errant tear as she and the mums of her cherished sleuths watched from the gallery as the girls proceeded up the hall to curtsey before the Queen. It was a bittersweet moment, knowing that this would be the last time this ball would take place. Eleanor had informed her that morning that the decision had been made. The ball no longer had a place in the more egalitarian world of the late 1950s. The world had changed, and the monarchy must too. Mary didn't need reminding that the world had changed.

Much of the money she'd earned training the girls was spent on Culpeper House, and though she expected some of that to be

covered by the Palace, there were still more repairs to the Snodsbury Estate to make.

During her farewell tea with Eleanor, Mary had gently
inquired, but the secretary was non-committal about future
commissions. She wasn't discouraging, so Mary hoped they were
considering her for something.

Ponsonby was waiting for her on her return, and she told
him briefly of their success.

"I'm most relieved to hear that, milady," he said as Cook
helped Mary to take off her coat. "Was the real princess there?"

"Sadly, no. The secret service felt they couldn't risk a reprisal
against her."

"I'm sorry such a fine tradition should end, but at least it
ended well," Ponsonby said.

Mary nodded. "Yes, it's fitting the last event should go
without a hitch. That way, the memories will be good ones."

"What do you have in mind now your commission is done,
milady?" Ponsonby asked as Mary set out for her room.

"Home, I think," Mary said, pausing at the foot of the stairs.
"We'll close up the London house and return to Snodsbury
Hall as soon as possible. I want to rid my mind of the horror
we've been part of, and a quiet spell in the country will do
that."

"Very good, milady," Ponsonby said, locking the doors and
preparing to make his nighttime inspection of windows. He
knew what she meant. The BBC news had reported on mass
arrests of many in Tzatzikistan over the past days, and he shared
her unhappiness in the part they'd played. "I'll begin the
removal first thing in the morning. I'll have the staff at Snodsbury begin preparing for our return."

"I have some small errands to run in town," Mary said. "I'll
travel after the reception in my honor at the Tzatzikistan
Embassy."

"I shall go on ahead then and leave you in Cook's care," Ponsonby said. "Good night, milady."

"DEAR OLD SNODSBURY," Mary said as the car rounded the bend and the view of the hall and grounds lay before her. She knocked on the window that separated her from Ponsonby, who'd met her and Cook at the station in the estate's old Rolls-Royce. "Stop, please. I want a moment to enjoy the view."

When the car rolled gently to a halt and was parked on the verge at the side of the road, she stepped out, carrying Barkley. Snodsbury looked lovely in the late evening sunshine. Its honey-colored stone shone like gold, and the gardens made a fresh green necklace around it. Trees were still in blossom, and nesting rooks swarmed around the old elms that provided a backdrop. She'd grown to love the hall through the years, maybe even more so after Roland died.

Mary wished there'd been children to carry on the line. As it was, some cousin who lived in Australia was to inherit when she was gone. Should she go now? Not "go" obviously. Just leave the hall and let the heir take early possession? It was too big for her, even with Ponsonby and Cook to help. She wished she knew more about the heir. Would he love it as she did or sell it for development the moment she was gone? She decided she must write and begin the process soon, for she wasn't growing any younger.

Mary turned back to the car as Ponsonby dutifully opened the passenger door. She slid into the seat, and the door closed. The decision not to hire permanent additional staff until she knew more about the Australian, but would bring in gardeners to recover some of the grounds, was forming in her mind. Maybe they could return the coverts to their rightful use and host shooting parties to raise cash. Ponsonby had suggested this to her years before, but her steward had pooh-poohed the notion as too expensive to set up.

"Glad to be home, milady?" Ponsonby asked as he held the door and she exited the car.

"It's good to be home," Mary said, nodding. "London is such a rackety place now. I'm sure it wasn't that way when I was younger."

"I'm sure you're right, milady. I thought the same myself," Ponsonby said as they walked together into the house.

"But London is more exciting than the country," Mary said wistfully. "I had a wonderful time at the Tzatzikistan Embassy Reception the other evening. Princess Jezebel, the real one this time and, by the way, the resemblance is remarkable, treated me royally."

"And her ankles, milady?"

Mary laughed. "Yes, Dotty was right. For such a dreamy, scatterbrained girl, she does see things that others miss."

"And the parcels in the boot, milady?" Ponsonby asked.

The local station's one porter had struggled to retrieve them from the train's luggage van and load them all on his trolley. It had taken Ponsonby some time to arrange them carefully in the car boot.

"The princess and new Tzatzikistan ambassador showered me with gifts, many of which I left at Culpeper."

"As they should, milady," Ponsonby said. "They owe you their lives."

"And they owe you too," Mary said.

"Cook and I also received gifts from the embassy only yesterday," Ponsonby said. "They're very fine. We're a little puzzled about how to acknowledge them. I'd like your advice on the matter. They may be too grand, and we should return them."

"Certainly not," Mary said sharply. "You and Cook were worth your weight in gold in this matter. Whatever it is, it's no more than you deserve."

"Then we shall make polite and appropriate replies," Ponsonby said. "I thought one of our professors may help with the words?"

"A simple English 'thank you' will be enough, and we can then forget the whole awful incident," Mary said brusquely. "Now, what's for dinner?"

Once again, Mary found her evening meal alone in Snodsbury Hall's dining room too sad and informed Ponsonby that she would eat dinner in the breakfast room in the future.

"Very well, milady," Ponsonby replied.

"Did I hear the telephone?"

"You did, milady. It was the chief superintendent. He will telephone again in an hour."

"Did he say what it was about?"

"I gather it was in relation to the MI5 man," Ponsonby said.

Griffiths was prompt to the time he'd given. "Good evening, Your Grace," he said when she picked up the phone.

"I do wish you'd stop that 'your grace' nonsense when we're alone," Mary said. "Mary is quite good enough."

"Ah, then I shall insist you drop Detective Chief Superintendent and call me Ivor."

"But I think of you as Detective Chief Superintendent," Mary said, "or at least Inspector." There was silence for a moment, and she said, "Very well, Ivor. What can you tell me about the man we knew as John."

"I have it on good assurance he will never be a problem, Mary," Griffiths said.

Mary shivered. "That's as ambiguous as their last statement, Ivor."

"That's all they will say," Griffiths replied. "You must take it for what it's worth."

"As you say," Mary replied, "and I will. Thank you for letting me know. I hope we have an opportunity to work together again soon."

"I hope so too," Griffiths replied, "and should you be in London again, perhaps we could meet without being part of an investigation?"

"I'd like that."

THREE MONTHS LATER, with summer drawing to a close, Mary, Barkley, and Ponsonby were standing on the terrace, looking out at the renovated rose gardens, and admiring the improvements her newly earned income was financing, for the Palace had finally paid most of the Culpeper improvement costs.

"Though I'm sorry about the death of Lady Hilary," Mary said, "I can't help thinking how fortunate it was for me and for Snodsbury Hall."

"It was, as you say, a dark cloud with a silver lining for all of us here at the hall," Ponsonby said.

"I heard from our sleuthing assistants this morning," Mary said. "I think they miss our company."

"They're very nice young women," Ponsonby said, though without much enthusiasm. "I hope they're all well?"

"They are," Mary said, "and they have a mystery to solve. They asked if they could meet with us at Culpeper House this weekend."

"And Snodsbury's beautiful new gardens?" Ponsonby asked innocently. "And the peace of the countryside?"

Mary smiled. "They will still be here when we return."

THE THREE YOUNG women who gathered around Lady Mary in Culpeper House's drawing room two days later looked, in Mary's eyes, transformed. Back in May, when she'd first seen them, they were pleasant yet gauche teenagers. Now, they were fine young women. She smiled and hoped her training had been part of the transformation.

"Sit down, ladies," Mary said, gesturing to the sofa and chairs. "We have a lot to talk about, and I have a lot to catch up on."

Barkley took this as an invitation for him to join them and sat watching with equal attention.

As usual, it was Winnie who began. "You do, and we want your advice."

"I gathered that from Margie's letter," Mary said. "You have a mystery at your home?" She directed her question to Margie.

"It's near my home," Margie said, "but it does affect my father in some way. He says not, and Mother says not, but it does."

"We've been staying at Margie's for the summer," Dotty interjected, "and sleuthing like mad."

"But without result," Winnie said, reasserting her place in the recital. "That's why we want your advice."

Mary looked at the three eager faces and nodded. "I see," she said. "You and whoever this mystery is affecting should tell the police, you know."

"Our local officer, Constable Watkins, is a nice man," Dotty said scornfully, "but he's no Sherlock Holmes."

"But he could bring in a detective from the county force," Mary said.

"He says he's explained to the county headquarters, and they say there's been no crime committed, and they won't intervene until there is," Margie said disgustedly.

"I see," Mary replied. "But you are all convinced there is something going on that will lead to a crime?"

"We are!" they cried excitedly, and for a moment, Mary could once again see the teenage girls they'd been when she first met them.

"I'll have Ponsonby organize drinks, and you can tell what you've discovered in all this sleuthing you've been doing." She rang the bell rope, and Ponsonby appeared almost immediately. "Ponsonby," Mary said, "we all need sherries, and you need to hear this strange tale as well."

With sherries in hand, they began their tale. When the three had finished speaking, they looked at Mary, waiting for her verdict.

"You've done well," Mary said, "and you gave your evidence well." She turned to Ponsonby who'd been listening intently and asked, "What's your opinion?"

"I believe our sleuths are right," he said. "The incidents are odd, and while apparently unconnected, there's something about them that isn't right."

"I agree," Mary said. "We should renew our sleuthing partnership."

"We need to have a name," Margie said, "like Enid Blyton's Famous Five, for instance."

"But there are six of us," Winnie said. "We three, Lady Mary, Ponsonby, and our leader—Barkley."

"Don't forget Cook," Margie said. "It was her brilliant tipping of glasses that allowed Lady Mary to get the brooch from the imposter."

"The Society of Six," Winnie said, "and a dog, Barkley, is still our leader." She stroked his head and gently tugged his ears.

Mary laughed. "The name needs work, I think, but for now, it must do."

"The Society of Six," Ponsonby said, raising his glass.

"Wait," Mary said. "We can't toast the new name with one of the Society missing."

She reached for the bell rope, but Ponsonby said, "She'll be in her precious new gardens. I'll go and find her."

Seeing the opportunity for action, Barkley leapt down from the couch and ran to the door.

"We'll all go," Mary said, "and take Cook's sherry with us."

Leave a review!

Thank you for reading our book!
We appreciate your feedback and love to
hear about how you enjoyed it!

Please leave a positive review letting us
know what you thought.

DUCHESS OF SNODSBURY TRILOGY

From the creative writers: P.C. James, author of the Best-Selling Miss Riddell Cozy Mystery Series and Kathryn Mykel, Award-Winning author of Best-Selling Sewing Suspicion, Quilting Cozy Mystery.

Royally Whacked

Royally Snuffed - Coming soon!

SASSY SENIOR SLEUTHS

Sassy Senior Sleuths

Sassy Senior Sleuths Return

Travel can be murder. Can Miss Riddell and Nona catch the villains before they become victims?

Travel forward from the Miss Riddell series to the twenty-first century with the demure Miss Pauline Riddell as she befriends a strangely lovable, fly by the seat of her pants amateur sleuth, named Gretta Galia aka Nona. The two sixty-five year-old travel companions visit tourist traps around the United States.

These stories move forward about twenty years from the Miss Riddell Series by P.C. James and back in time about twenty years from the Quilting Cozy Mystery series by Kathryn Mykel. Approximating the setting of these stories to be during the turn of the 21st century, between 2000-2005.

Join us in the Adventures of Pauline and Nona Facebook group and let us know you've read the story, what you think of this quick mini mystery; and if you made the recipe! https://www.facebook.com/groups/paulineandnona/

From the creative writers: P.C. James, author of the Best-Selling Miss Riddell Cozy Mystery Series and Kathryn Mykel, author of Best-Selling Sewing Suspicion A Quilting Cozy Mystery Series.

ABOUT THE AUTHOR P.C. JAMES

P.C. James, Author of the Miss Riddell Series

I've always loved mysteries, especially those involving Agatha Christie's Miss Marple. Perhaps because Miss Marple reminded me of my aunts when I was growing up. But Christie never told us much about Miss Marple's earlier life. When writing my own elderly super-sleuth series, I'm tracing her career from the start. As you'll see, if you follow the Miss Riddell Cozy Mysteries over the coming years.

However, this is my Bio, not Miss Riddell's, so here goes with all you need to know about me: After retiring, I became a writer and, as a writer, I spend much of my day staring at the computer screen hoping inspiration will strike. I'm pleased to say, it eventually does. For the rest, you'll find me running, cycling, walking, and taking wildlife photos wherever and whenever I can. My cozy mystery series begins in northern England because that was my home growing up and that's also the home of so many great cozy mysteries. Stay with me though because Miss Riddell loves to travel as much as I do and the stories will take us to many different places around the world.

- Facebook: https://www.facebook.com/ PCJamesAuthor
- Bookbub: https://www.bookbub.com/authors/p-c-james
- Amazon Author Page: https://www.amazon.com/P.-C.-James/e/B08VTN7Z8Y

- GoodReads Page: https://www.goodreads.com/author/show/20856827.P_C_James
- Amazon Series Page: My Book
- Miss Riddell Newsletter signup: https://landing.mailerlite.com/webforms/landing/x7a9e4

Books on Amazon:

In the Beginning, There Was a Murder

Then There Were ... Two Murders?

The Past Never Dies

A Murder for Christmas

Miss Riddell and the Heiress

Miss Riddell's Paranormal Mystery

The Girl in the Gazebo

The Dead of Winter

It's Murder, on a Galapagos Cruise

ABOUT THE AUTHOR KATHRYN MYKEL

Kathryn Mykel, author of Sewing Suspicion - A Quilting
Inspired by the laugh-out-loud and fanciful aspects of cozies, Kathryn Mykel aims to write lighthearted, humorous cozies surrounding her passion for the craft of quilting.

Kathryn is an avid quilter, born and raised in a small New England town. She enjoys writing cozy mysteries and sweet, clean romances.

For more fun quilt fiction cozy reads and new releases, sign up for her newsletter or join her and her Readers on Facebook at Author Kathryn Mykel or Books For Quilters For more quilt fiction in the Sweet Romance Genre you can find her on Facebook at Author Kathryn LeBlanc or on her books on Amazon.

- Newsletter signup: https://view.flodesk.com/pages/618e6d793a0e5bcf6f541be1
- Bookbub https://www.bookbub.com/profile/kathryn-mykel
- GoodReads Page: https://www.goodreads.com/author/show/21921434.Kathryn_Mykel
- Website: https://SewingSuspicion.mailerpage.com

Quilting Cozy Mystery Reads on Amazon:
Sewing Suspicion
Quilting Calamity
Pressing Matters
Mutterly Mistaken

Threading Trouble

Sweet Romance Reads on Amazon:
Quinn: Runaway Brides of the West
Christmas Star Cottage
Sugar Cookie Inn

Printed in Great Britain
by Amazon